Twisting and weaving crazily, flaps down to reduce their speed to almost stalling, the cannonbirds came in time and time again, mindless of the flak, hurtling through the fire-red mesh of anti-aircraft fire, pressing home their attack with the bravery and recklessness of the good days, when nothing in the world had been able to stop the all-conquering *blitzkrieg*.

Also by Leo Kessler

and published by Corgi Books

SS Stuka Squadron 3:
Tank-Busters!

Leo Kessler

CORGI BOOKS

SS STUKA SQUADRON 3: TANK-BUSTERS!
A CORGI BOOK 0 552 12407 9

Originally published in Great Britain by
Century Publishing Co. Ltd.

PRINTING HISTORY
Century edition published 1984
Corgi edition published 1984

This book is set in Baskerville 10/11 pt.

Corgi Books are published by
Transworld Publishers Ltd.,
Century House, 61–63 Uxbridge Road,
Ealing, London W5 5SA

Printed and bound in Great Britain by
Cox & Wyman Ltd., Reading

'STUKA ... STUKA ... STUKA!
Hawks of death ... Death is our companion,
blood our colour, steel our weapon!
STUKA ... STUKA ... STUKA!'

The Battle Song of the 1st SS Stuka Squadron

PART ONE

Death on the Dnieper

CHAPTER 1

THE GREY mist rolled in from the river across the icy white waste. Here and there a smudge of brown earth indicated a German position. Tracks leading to the snow-heavy fir woods showed where the Tigers and Mark IVs had gone into hiding. A couple of heavy gun batteries were visible, their crews shivering beneath the white camouflage netting.

Major de la Mazière, second-in-command of the 1st SS Stuka Group, nodded his approval and swept round in a slow curve, his own group of twenty-seven Stukas following. To his left and right, Captain Hanno von Heiter and Lieutenant Baron Karst did the same with their groups. Now, nearly a hundred Stukas were in position, circling the battlefield like sinister black hawks, waiting.

Above the circle of Stukas, C.O. Colonel Greim dog-legged back and forth in his Messerschmitt 110, watching his young bloods of the SS with a worried look on his scarred face. He knew his 'black aristocrats', as they were nicknamed by the Luftwaffe ground crews. As usual they were out for glory and fame, and the 'tin'* which went with it. They damn well needed watching.'

The ranks of the élite 1st SS Group were packed with raw kids of eighteen and nineteen, straight from the training schools of the Reich, full of piss and vinegar. They still believed the Stuka to be the invincible weapon of terror—'the Führer's flying artillery'—it had been in the great days of 1940. They didn't know that the Stuka was at least a hundred kilometres an hour slower than the average Ivan fighter and no match for the mobile flak that every Ivan division possessed these days. If he, Greim, was going to bring them

*SS slang for decorations and medals awarded for bravery

back alive from what was soon to come, he'd need to wet nurse them and powder their skinny SS arses exceedingly carefully. Colonel Greim flew on, eyes searching the fog to the east from which they would come. Soon!

Flying to de la Mazière's port, Hanno von Heiter stroked Fifi's comforting fur. As the silly little French poodle crouched next to him in the tight cockpit, her owner's red-rimmed drunkard's gaze peered desperately into the grey gloom. As always, he was terribly afraid, the hand that held the controls shaking visibly. He licked his lips and wished he could put a good belt of vodka behind his collar to steady his nerves. His heart was thumping like an Ivan Maxim firing all-out. He seemed to be flying through a gloomy grey cavern of fog, here and there a funereal light penetrating it in chinks, the dangers below still mercifully blotted out. But for how long, he asked himself fearfully. *For how shitting long?* Heaven, arse and cloudburst, he'd give his right arm at this moment for a snort of fire-water!

'Sir!' Sergeant Hannemann's gruff voice broke into his frightened reverie.

'Yes, Hannemann,' he replied over the intercom to the gunner crouching behind him. 'Where's the fire now?'

'Right behind us, sir,' Hannemann growled in his tough Berlin manner. 'One of those piss pansies they call pilots these days is almost sticking his nose up our ass. Can't yer warn him off, sir, before he shafts us?'

'Those piss pansies, Hannemann, I must remind you,' said von Heiter, with a trace of the old humour which had once made him the First's comedian before he had lost his nerve, 'are all officers and gentlemen. I trust that you will select more suitable—'

—'Tiger One to all!' Greim's voice cut into von Heiter's words urgently. 'Tiger One to all. . . . Here they come. . . . Are you reading me? *HERE THEY COME!*'

Von Heiter gasped. Next to him, Fifi tensed. As if by

magic, the fog had opened up to reveal what they had been waiting for.

Massed tanks were waddling out of the river like clumsy metallic ducks, the snow spraying up behind them. Then came the infantry, row after row trampling solidly forward as if on parade on Red Square, their bayonets gleaming in the thin grey light: a huge block of marching men stretching to the horizon.

Behind von Heiter, Hannemann craned his neck and said in an awed whisper, 'Holy strawsack, Major. . . . *It's the whole of the shitting Popov Army!*'

Lieutenant Baron Karst's icy-blue eyes narrowed as he surveyed that awesome spectacle. At three o'clock there was a group of flak wagons: old tanks with their turrets removed and now mounting four high-speed flak cannon, each one capable of firing a thousand shells a minute. It would be sheer suicide to attack in that direction, he told himself. Leave the flak wagons to that fool von Heiter, or de la Mazèire, who had usurped his own rightful position as second-in-command.* If they wanted to risk their famous necks doing so, the best of luck to them. He would tackle the first line of tanks. In and out, before the Popov gunners had time to line him up in their sights. He pressed his intercom.

'Tiger Three to all!' he commanded in his harsh nasal voice, 'Attacking . . . attacking . . . Follow me . . . *SIEG HEIL!*'

The bold greeting was echoed by a score of hoarsely exuberant young throats, as Baron Karst threw his plane out of the sky and commenced that tremendous ride of the Valkyries yet again.

Sirens screaming, the wind howling through the air brakes, the engines racing all out, the Black Knights of the 1st SS Stuka Group fell from the heavens. At an impossibly crazy speed they hurtled down towards the attacking Russians. The

*See *Hawks of War* for further details

ground leapt up to meet them. One after the other they
followed each other on that wild, suicidal helter-skelter. The
battle for the river crossing had started.

All that winter they had been retreating. Stop, dig in, wait,
defend, a stand made for a few days, a few hours, and they
would be off again, hounded by the grey horde of the 'Ivans',
leaving yet another bunch of 'stiffs' behind them to disappear
under the snow of those trackless steppes, never again to see
their homeland. All winter.

It had been one 'strategic withdrawal' after another for the
hard-pressed men of the 'Greater German Wehrmacht',
which had never known defeat. Along the 2000-mile front in
Russia, stretching from the Gulf of Finland in the north to the
Black Sea in the south, the Red Army rolled inexorably
forward.

Once, given a few days' breathing space, the Führer had
ordered a counter-attack from Minsk. It had run head-on
into an impenetrable wall of Russian resistance. For six long
bloody miles the Germans had staggered forward, every mile
costing the Army thousands of casualties and hundreds of
armoured vehicles, before falling to a halt like a punch-drunk
bruiser dropping to his knees for a count of nine. A day later
the 'Ivans' had attacked again in force and the 'strategic
withdrawals' had commenced once more.

Now the weary, lousy, half-starved field-greys no longer
talked of 'strategic withdrawals'. They talked of 'flight' and
downright 'running away'. They were fleeing from the
Russian bear! Men and tanks swarmed back to the west,
driven on by the knowledge that the Cossacks, with their
cruel knouts and blood-red sabres, were waiting for
stragglers, streaming across that snowy waste like a river
which had broken its banks, followed by the persistent
rumbling of the permanent barrage. Men in panic, men at
the end of their tether, men who had gone crazy, men who

dropped sobbing to the snow, unable to continue, pleading piteously with their comrades to shoot them, to put an end to their misery. '*SHOOT ME, COMRADE . . . SHOOT . . . PL . . . EASE . . .!*'

The retreat became a rout. Now it was the accursed Ivans who used the *blitzkrieg* tactics they had perfected in France back in that glorious summer of 1940. Stormovik dive-bombers came barrelling in, machine-guns chattering, bombs howling down. By their hundreds, their thousands, the T-34s with the hated, red star on their turrets came rattling across the snow, cannon roaring, flame throwers hissing, smashing, burning, over-running everything before them. Infantry followed, division after division, crying their dread, bass '*Urrah*' as they stomped into battle in massed ranks, shoulder to shoulder, sometimes ten deep, their brass bands playing, as if in celebration.

Nothing seemed able to stop them. They drove the leaderless, broken German formations before them across that endless steppe. Horch staff cars, eight-ton trucks, caterpillar tractors, tanks, ammo trucks, little horse-drawn, looted *panje* wagons. They skidded and lurched ever onwards, sliding on that treacherous snow and ice, drivers gunning their engines, eyes wild with fear, hands frozen to the wheels, hearts racing as they waited for that great animal cheer and the clatter and thunder of Cossack hooves as they raced across the snow to slaughter the 'Fritzes'. On and on, their progress marked by the litter of field-grey bodies, sprawled on the wayside like pathetic, abandoned broken dolls, and the blood-red faeces of those suffering from dysentery.

Now the rout became a debacle. The thaw of 1943 had come with startling suddenness. The snow gave way to thick black mud. Vehicles sank ankle-deep into the muck. Drivers and vehicles were covered with it, as they fought and slithered their way through. The headlong retreat slowed to a miserable, frightened crawl. Cossacks and partisans were everywhere. Men were shot, trapped to their waists in the quagmire. Stragglers were cut off, tortured, crucified to barn doors, run through circular saws, hung upside down from telegraph poles, their sliced-off genitals thrust mockingly into their gaping mouths.

Some of the fleeing men went mad. Others shot off their toes through loaves of bread to prevent tell-tale powder burns and tried to get themselves evacuated—in time. Many simply cut their own throats with their issue razors and bled to death. The officers tried to prevent the rot from spreading. They were a thousand kilometres from home, cut off in this awesome alien world. What if the whole army broke down? It would be the beginning of the end. The exodus was a miserable shambles, dominated by panic, driven by fear. The most powerful Army the world had ever known was disintegrating before their very eyes. It had to be stopped! Before it was too late.

'*Reach the Dnieper*,' they urged. 'Once we gain the river, we stop and push them back. . . . There are prepared defences there. . . . Reserves. . . . New formations. . . . Whole armoured divisions. . . . Bunkers. . . . Built-up stop lines. . . .' They pleaded over and over again. 'Just reach the Dnieper, boys, and we are safe . . . *the Dnieper, that's all*. . . .'

But there were no built-up defences on the great Russian river which rolled like a sluggish grey snake through the mire and the melting snowfields, no bunkers, no armoured divisions, no new formations. Nothing to fall back on—save one thing. Colonel Greim's 1st SS Stuka Group . . . *the Stukas of the Black Guards*!

De la Mazière groaned. Baron Karst's number two had been hit. Quite distinctly he could see the plane stagger, as a violet fire-ball exploded at his nearside wing. De la Mazière held his breath, his own dive momentarily forgotten, as the young pilot, a kid of eighteen and still wet behind the spoons, tried to hold the stricken plane. To no avail! His wing flew off, fluttering down like an autumn leaf, as more and more mobile flak peppered the sky about the Stukas, first black and then pale grey. The plane went into its last dive. At 400 kilometres an hour, it raced to the ground. The Ivans scrambled to get out of its way as it hurtled towards them, trailing thick black smoke, flecked with bright orange flame.

At 500 kilometres an hour, it slammed into the earth. A tremendous explosion. Even de la Mazière could feel the impact. He gripped the controls with hands that were wet with sweat. The Stuka disintegrated, on wheel sailing lazily into the air beyond the pall of smoke.

That first hit seemed to signal the mass slaughter of the Stukas, as they came screaming in for the kill and the mobile flak cannon took up the challenge. Abruptly the sky was a network of blazing red and white tracer, spotted everywhere with the black puffballs of exploding shells. Plane after plane was hit. Suddenly, on all sides, they were soaring into their death dives, trailing that awesome last funereal smoke, parachutes blossoming in white bursts as the young pilots attempted to escape before it was too late.

Baron Karst broke off just in time. The damned flak had found him quicker than he had anticipated. His eyes icy cold and calculating, he hurled the Stuka into a wild curve, searching the battlefield below for easy targets, noting that on the German side of the Dnieper the survivors of the great retreat had come out of their hiding places and were fighting back. The river was shrouded in gunsmoke, pierced by the urgent lethal morse of tracer. The battle was hotting up.

Again Karst circled, followed by his obedient wing-man, who was undoubtedly wondering why his superior did not plunge into the attack like the others. Let him wonder, the young fool, Karst told himself. He, too, was of the old aristocracy, another of those who had joined the SS, not out of belief in the Holy Creed of National Socialism, but because the Black Guards offered quick promotion and a chance to restore the tarnished reputation of his impoverished family.

He was like the rest. Karst's thin cruel lips curled in contempt. They were opportunists all of them, and that included de la Mazière and von Heiter. His own family were different. The Karsts had *worked* for their title, coming up from the foundry floor until they owned a whole steel works, just as he, three generations later, was working hard to re-establish the name of the family, firm in the belief that National Socialism was the creed of the future. Suddenly he spotted his target.

'Tiger Three. . . . Tiger Three!' he called urgently to those of his group who still survived. 'Stalled Infantry . . . ten o'clock. . . . Bunching nicely.' He waggled his wings, while his wing-man and the others hovered in the air. Karst took a deep breath, and a last haughty arrogant glance at his Stukas. '*Attacking!*' He pushed the stick over fiercely. '*NOW!*'

The Stuka fell out of the sky. Sirens screaming, it hurtled towards the grey mass of Russian infantry, hundreds, perhaps thousands of them, crowded together, a perfect target. Behind him his gunner, Sergeant 'Slack Arse' Schmidt, gasped. 'Why don't the Popov yo-yos get out of the way? It's gonna be sheer slaughter! What shitting idiots they are, sir!'

Karst didn't answer. His attention was concentrated on the target, his face set in a mask of death. Now as the ground rushed up to meet him at an alarming rate, he shot a quick glance at the flickering green needle of his altimeter . . . *5,000 metres . . . 4,500 . . . 4,000 . . . 2,000 . . . 1,000 . . .*

The plane creaked and shrieked under the pressure. Karst choked for breath. Blood thundered at his temples. There were strange popping noises in his ears. A red veil spread before his eyes. Cruel fingers twisted his guts. His cheekbones seemed to thrust iron skewers into his eyes. Blood began to spurt thick and red from his nostrils and ears. *Five hundred metres!*

'By the Great Whore of Buxtehude, sir!' Slack Arse screamed with fear. 'Drop the eggs, sir. . . . *Drop the shitting eggs!*' At the last moment Karst fought off the red mist which threatened to swamp him. He hit the rudder-bar, hard. In the same instant he pressed the toggle. The Stuka reared up a good twenty-five metres as it was freed of its load and the deadly black eggs started to tumble towards the stalled Russian infantry.

For a moment Karst blacked out under that tremendous pressure, thrust back against his seat by the G-force, eyes bulging out of his sweat-lathered, crimson face like those of a madman.

'My God, sir, you've got the Popov shits! *You've got 'em!*' Slack Arse Schmidt's crazy yell of triumph brought him to his senses again. Below, the bombs ran the length of the Russians. They couldn't miss. Great blood-red gaps, shrouded by the black smoke of explosive, appeared in their ranks. Bodies flew through the air. In a flash, the scene became a chaotic carnage of dying, maimed, terribly mutilated young men. Those who could flung away their weapons in unreasoning panic and fled screaming across the fields in an attempt to escape those crows of death.

Karst sobbed hysterically. In the moment that he regained control of the plane, he screamed as if in the throes of sexual pleasure, a strange weakness flooding his loins, and soared high into the sky, away from the battle. Let the fools die. He, the Fourth Baron Karst, was going to *live . . . live . . . live*. Down below, the twitching dying bodies piled high like cordwood.

Colonel Greim cursed, as he circled once again, surveying that terrible scene of death. Karst had gone for the wrong target. Why in three devils' name had he picked the soft option—the foot soldiers—when the Russian T-34s were still plunging forward unharmed? Damn the arrogant Nazi bastard! He always thought of himself and his own advantage. If the Russian tanks, crawling ever nearer to the poor, wretched stubble-hoppers of the German Front, were not stopped immediately, then it would be all over. The Line of the Dnieper would break and the Army would be on the run again. He pressed his R/T button. Throwing all SOP* to the winds, he cried urgently, 'De la Mazière, are you reading me? De la Mazière, come in, for God's sake! Over!'

De la Mazière answered almost immediately and Greim could tell, in spite of the chatter of machine-guns and the metallic distortion, that the handsome young blond aristocrat with the harsh face was almost at the end of his tether. Instinctively he knew that his Group had already taken severe casualties.

'De la Mazière,' he barked, trying to put iron into his voice, though he hated what he was going to have to do to de la Mazière and his survivors. 'Max effort. . . . Knock out that leading wave of T-34s. It's imperative. If you don't, God only knows what—' He broke off.

'But sir,' de la Mazière's voice, distorted as it was, was full of urgent pleading. 'I've already lost half of them. They're so green . . . and the shitting Stuka is simply too shitting old for this kind of fighting. . . . Sir, they're only kids,' he ended lamely. 'Over.'

'Obey my command, Major!' Greim forced himself to be harsh and overbearing. 'Or take the consequences. Now knock out that lead-wave.' Greim flung a glance over the side of his cockpit and saw line after line of T-34s scuttling ever closer to the waiting German infantry, their long, overhanging 75mm cannon already spouting death and destruction. 'It is imperative. Over and out!'

For one long moment Greim thought his young second-in-command was going to disobey him. But 200 years of service to the German state and iron military discipline triumphed. '*Zu befehl, Herr Oberst!*' de la Mazière answered with the stiff Prussian bark of his ancestors, '*Over and out!*'

*Standard Operating Procedure

CHAPTER 2

'CORPORAL,' de la Mazière snapped, efficient and business-like now, as what was left of his Group—ten planes in all—assembled around him, high above the battlefield.

'Sir!' his young gunner answered, fear in his voice. He had left gunnery school back in the Reich only two months before and had never anticipated that aerial combat in the famed Stuka would be like this.

'Keep your eyes absolutely peeled,' de la Mazière barked, waiting impatiently while his young hawks made ready. 'Don't worry about what's going on on the ground. Leave that to me. Watch the east. As soon as you spot one of their fighters, sing out. *Clear?*'

'Clear, sir?' the gunner quavered.

De la Mazière forced a cheerful note. 'Don't worry, Corporal. I've been in this business since the beginning. And apart from a few odd scratches, the only serious thing that has happened to me is that I've got piles from sitting on these awful shitting seats! All right?'

'All right, sir.' Behind him the tousle-haired teenager managed a frightened smile. The handsome young hero up front in his jaunty black leather jacket, the Knight's Cross hanging at his throat, was a good chap, in spite of what the other Luftwaffe gunners said about these black aristocrats. He knew how to talk to the ordinary airman. He forgot his fears and gripped the handle of the machine gun, eyes searching the grey horizon to the east with renewed energy.

De la Mazière forgot the gunner. 'Tiger Two to all,' he commanded. 'We shall attack in the chain. Present the smallest target that way. Right up tight next to each other's arsehole. One time—and one time only. Remember you have to be right on target. No near misses. Then your bombs will have no effect on the top armour of those damned T-34s. And one last thing. As soon as anyone sights a fighter, *scramble*! Hug the ground and head for home with yer feet under your arms.' He forced a laugh. 'You are absolutely no match whatsoever for the Ivan Yaks. All right, comrades. Here we go. *An alle! Hals und Beinbruch!*'* He thrust the stick forward.

Gripping the shuddering controls with all his strength, de la Mazière watched as the earth spun round and round below and the green needles on the control panel oscillated crazily. He gasped for breath, carried away by the old, wild excitement of the kill. How many times had he done this— in France, Belgium, Greece, Jugoslavia, Crete and now Russia—and always that heady, death-defying dive had thrilled him with its mad exhilaration! Again he fought the seductive temptation to surrender to the force of nature dragging him downwards to plummet to his destruction. Instead he sought his target, a cluster of T-34s, led by a command tank—he knew that from the tiny black figure of the commander wagging his flags. Ideal! If he could knock that one out, the rest would be lost. Without an efficient radio communication system between tanks, once their commander was lost, the usual Russian armoured force went to pieces.

The earth and those grey metallic slugs were racing up to meet him. He could see the surrounding infantry diving crazily for cover or flinging away their rifles to race into the fields. His jaw tightened. His thumb sought the bomb toggle. '*Now!*' he croaked through gritted teeth, feeling the sweat pour in rivulets down his strained, crimson face, and pressed the button.

The Stuka leapt. For a moment he almost lost control. It surged forward at an even greater speed. De la Mazière grabbed it just in time before it went into its last dive. He hit the brakes and jerked back the stick with all his strength, his

---

*Literally, 'Break your neck and legs'. Equivalent of 'Happy landings'

shoulder muscles ablaze with the strain and threatening to burst the thin material of his shirt. The fuselage trembled like a wild animal trapped for the first time. He opened his mouth instinctively and found himself screaming. His eardrums were about to burst. Red and white stars exploded before his eyes. Then he had her once more, every rivet howling with that almost unbearable strain, and he was surging high into the sky, effortlessly, followed by the angry black puffballs of the flak. *He had done it!* His bomb had landed smack on the target. Below the command tank lay wrecked and smoking, its long cannon hanging limply like a broken head.

As the T-34s scuttled about in complete disorganisation, de la Mazière's young pilots came falling out of the grey sky, sirens howling, air-brakes screeching, to drop their own bombs. Tank after tank went up in flames, the gas exploding instantly, searing the length of the stalled metal monsters in a great roaring blowtorch. Suddenly all was thunder, the whooshing of flame, the terrifying metallic creak as the tanks reeled and died under those tremendous hammerblows.

Shocked, white-faced, screaming tankers scrambled from their stricken vehicles, their hands already claws of blue flame, dropping to the ground to twist and turn as the fire consumed them, their struggles weaker by the second.

The Germans rose from their foxholes. Whistles shrilled. Officers bellowed orders. Red-faced noncoms screamed and kicked the laggards. Carried away by the bloodlust and mad fury of battle, they streamed forward, bodies bent against the hail of Soviet fire like men struggling through torrential rain. Ignoring the whirling maelstrom of flying steel, they slammed into the stalled Russians.

Machine guns chattered. Everywhere the running men went down, spines arched grotesquely in the ecstasy of death, hands clawing the air in one last attempt to stave it off. But still the others came on, fighting and stumbling over the twitching bodies of their comrades, which lay on the way to the river like a grey carpet.

The infantry surged between the burning T-34s. The surviving crew members were slaughtered where they lay, slain like dumb animals, without the strength to plead for mercy.

On and on they rushed. They slammed into the stalled ranks of the Russian foot soldiers, taken by surprise at this sudden animal fury. The battlefield broke into small swirling groups of Russian and German infantrymen. It was man to man, atavastic, primeval. No quarter given or expected. When a man went down, he did not rise again. Mercilessly they slashed, gouged, hacked, chopped, gasping like asthmatics, faces glazed with sweat, mouthing obscenities, wading through an ankle-deep red slush of their own blood. The tanks, the planes, the guns, all those man-made weapons of war were forgotten. It was the instinct of the caveman which now dominated the battlefield, an impulse that could only be sated by blood, gore, and violent death.

High above, Colonel Greim, veteran of three wars, knew his men had pulled it off. They had accomplished the impossible, though they had paid severely in doing so—in stopping the Russian advance. The line of the Dnieper would hold—for a while. He stared at the terrible lunar landscape, his planes wrecked and burning on all sides, here and there a handful peeling off like black tulips opening their petals, going into death-defying dives yet again, as the lethal, feathery black flak peppered the sky. His young aristocrats had suffered enough. This spring day they had settled the butcher's bill.

It was time to get the survivors home before the fighters arrived. He pressed his R/T button. 'Tiger One to all,' he said with sudden weariness, suddenly feeling the ache in his bones and reminding himself he was getting too old for this sort of thing. It was time he became a rear echelon stallion and started to polish a nice comfortable chair back in Berlin and ogle the 'grey mice' in their too-tight skirts.* 'Return to

---

*Nickname for the female military auxiliaries

base. Ret—' He stopped abruptly, his ears full of the urgent cackle of an over-excited operator far to the rear, repeating their call-sign over and over again.

He pressed 'Receive' and listened aghast to what the operator had to say. Immediately the message was over, he hit R/T himself once more and rapped, forgetting standard operating procedure in his haste, using clear. 'Greim to all. Break up! Break up! Make for Morosovskaya Field! Home base at Tazinskaya under attack! Do you read me, pilots? *Do not land at Tazinskaya!* It is already probably in enemy hands.'

He flashed a look at his fuel gauge. The green needle was already edging perilously close to 'E',* as must be all their needles. The whole damned Group was running out of gas. 'Break and head for Morosovskaya! *Over and out!*' The battle for the river crossing forgotten, aware that it was every man for himself and that any pilot who fell into Soviet hands hadn't a chance in hell of surviving, especially after today, Colonel Greim flung his fighter into a long banking dive. He was going home, *tootsweet!*

'Did I ever tell you, sir, about the bit of gash I had once in Smolensk who had four tits?'

Hanno von Heiter dived ever lower as the Stukas scuttled for home, and Hannemann started to reminisce.

'A real old Popov juicy Lucy she was. Could have put yer head between the top pair and never heard a thing for a couple of weeks or so—they were that big!'

Hannemann swung a controlled look from left to right. The grey sky, flecked here and there by the mushrooms of black smoke rising above the Dnieper, was empty of Ivan fighters. 'Then she had this other pair a couple of centimetres lower—kind of a reserve set o' tits, as you might say—'

Hanno von Heiter sighed and pressed Fifi's skinny, furry

*Empty

body for reassurance; once more his little mascot had brought him through safely. But for how much longer? Once he lost Fifi, he knew he'd be finished. Without his mascot he hadn't a chance.

'Senior Sergeant Hannemann,' he said firmly. I must have you know I've not experienced a real bone between my legs since we last hit the knocking shops on leave in Berlin—and that's a good six moons ago. So, can't you, my dear senior sergeant, talk about something else?'

'Of course, sir,' Hannemann replied obligingly. 'What about dogs? I can talk about hounds.'

He stared at the back of von Heiter's neck. It was wet with sweat, and he knew why. The handsome young officer with the drinker's face was scared. He always was these days. Only his stupid frog pooch and the daily bottle of firewater kept him going. Once Hannemann had feared and hated those arrogant young 'black aristocrats' who had lorded it over him and the other 'peasants' of the Luftwaffe's NCO Corps. Now he could feel sorry for such as von Heiter, survivors whose nerve had gone. But still he had to keep his eye on the new shits, those greenbeaks from the training schools, still wet behind the spoons. They were as arrogant as the old ones had once been, out for glory and promotion at the expense of the poor shitting air gunners such as Frau Hannemann's handsome son.

Von Heiter patted Fifi once more. His fuel tank was almost empty, he noted, but he'd make the alternative field all right. He flashed a look in his rear-view mirror. The silver square of gleaming glass was empty. Not an enemy fighter in sight. 'Yes,' he said, beginning to relax. 'Talk about dogs, if you must, Hannemann.'

'Well, they're different from pigeons, for a start,' Hannemann humoured him, noting that the rest of the group had vanished into the cloud below. 'If you feed pigeons, they end up by crapping on yer.'

Von Heiter laughed hollowly. 'Well said, Senior Sergeant

Hannemann!' He brought the Stuka ever lower so that it dragged its evil black shadow across the belt of clouds below. 'Well said, indeed!'

'And besides,' Hannemann continued, a roguish look in his faded blue eyes, 'if you get hungry, you can eat 'em. Dogs I mean.'

'What in the three devils' name did you say?' von Heiter rapped, shocked.

'Eat 'em!' Hannemann chuckled. 'They're a lot tastier than roof-hare.* Yer average roof-hare's got a dry sort o' taste, whereas yer roasted dog is much more juicy. I remember back in Spain in the old days of the Condor Legion,** we was once—' He broke off suddenly; the mocking look vanished from his big tough face, his eyes became watchful. A sinister black spot had appeared in the sky behind them—and it was growing larger by the second! He swallowed hard and felt an icy finger of fear trace its way unpleasantly down his spine.

Hanno von Heiter flew on, unaware of the danger approaching so swiftly. Hannemann swung round his single machine-gun to meet the challenge, hoping against hope that he was wrong and the speck was simply another Stuka, a straggler like themselves. But that wasn't to be. There was no mistaking that stubby, round-barrelled shape with the short clipped wings.

'Sir,' he sang out urgently, 'bandit twelve o'clock high! YAK, I think, sir!'

Von Heiter's heart missed a beat. For a moment he was frozen to the controls, unable to look in the mirror. 'Definite, sir!' Hannemann cried, clicking back his bolt as the enemy fighter approached, narrowing the gap between himself and the slow, ponderous dive-bomber at an alarming rate. He started to draw a bead on the Yak, tensing his body for the

*Slang for 'cat'
**German 'volunteer' formation which fought on General Franco's side in the Spanish Civil War

violent aerial manoeuvres that von Heiter would be forced to make, if they were going to get out of this one. And he'd better act soon, or Frau Hannemann's son would be right up to his hooter in crap—as per usual!

Von Heiter flashed a look upwards, just as the violet angry lights flared the length of the enemy fighter's stubby wings. Tracer zapped towards his plane, converging ever more rapidly, as if to trap him between those lines of death.

Von Heiter froze. He was paralysed to the marrow of his bones with fright. Hannemann shouted over the intercom. A hot flush swept through his body. The instinct of self-preservation returned. Fifi yelped as he kicked the rudder bar. Stick to the left in one swift movement. He almost passed out with the violence of the manoeuvre. A black mist threatened to engulf him. Something ripped the length of the fuselage. He could smell the acridity of burnt explosive.

The next moment the fat little Yak fighter swept by, harmlessly, and Hannemann was firing a furious burst at its vanishing tail. Now he was on his back, flying just above the cloud. Another Yak zoomed by, helpless to attack him. Von Heiter reacted instinctively, adrenalin spurting crazily into his blood stream. He jerked the stick and straightened out. To his front, he caught a glimpse of the first Yak tearing round in a terrific curve, trying to swing back into the attack before he, Hanno, could reach the cover of the clouds. 'That'll be the day!' he cried triumphantly, in spite of his fear. He hit his own firing button. The twin machine guns mounted in the wings burst into frenetic life. Fifi howled, but Hanno von Heiter had no time for his mascot now. Straightening out the ailerons, he hurtled vertically for the clouds.

'Saved!' he yelled, as the Stuka sank into the thick comforting white mass. 'Now find me, you Popov piss pansy!'

'*Richtig!*' Hannemann howled in agreement, as von Heiter started to change course every three seconds, knowing that one of the Yaks would be tailing him somewhere in the clouds, the other flying just above cloud-base waiting for him to emerge into the clear. It was an old fighter trick—and he, Hanno von Heiter, was not playing it this day, no sir! *He was going to survive.* . . .

It was the same promise that de la Mazière was making to himself that very moment, some ten kilometres away, as the squadron of Yaks came racing in in that strange irregular formation they always used, dancing up and down in the grey sky like ugly, awkward porpoises.

To his front, his stragglers and those of the other two groups panicked. The first Yak made a kill. There was a muted chatter of machine guns and then a Stuka fell out of the sky, spurting white glycol vapour.

'Jump! For God's sake, *jump!*' de la Mazière cried to himself in a frenzy of horror, as the Stuka started to roar to its destruction.

A figure hurled through the sky in front of him, head tucked well in, hands clasped to bent knees like a super acrobat. A white parachute blossomed and the Stuka pilot was swaying back and forth gently, his mad flight through the heavens brought to a sudden halt.

De la Mazière's harshly handsome face lit up. But not for long. Another Yak was racing in, its machine guns blazing at the lone pilot trapped in mid-sky. '*No!*' de la Mazière shrieked, as the cruel fire ripped into the youth, leaving him swaying lifelessly.

He forgot his own danger. He urged his plane forward, almost physically like a jockey, face contorted with rage, eyes blazing. He hit the firing button. The range was extreme, but he was too angry to care. There was a swordthrust of white gleaming tracer, an angry flash that rippled the length of the Yak. Angry flames started almost immediately. The Russian lost control. The Yak flipped over on its back and screamed earthwards. No one bailed out.

Almost immediately two of the Russian fighters turned

their attention to the new victim. They broke off from the slaughter of the stragglers, zooming upwards, trailing brown smoke through the grey sky and then peeled off to left and right.

De la Mazière opened his throttle, and threw the Stuka into a steep climb. The tactic completely surprised the nearest Yak pilot. Obviously he had thought the German would head for the cover of the clouds. He did not live to regret his oversight.

He opened fire, but de la Mazière was already gone. The slugs zipped harmlessly far below. De la Mazière levelled out. Behind him his corporal yelled in alarm, but the pilot did not hear. He was too concerned with the kill and the fact that the G-force was slamming him back into the seat, nearly punching his guts through his spine. He commenced a tight turn.

The Yak tried to turn inside him. In vain. De la Mazière had the advantage, until it began to stall. In a flash it was spinning downwards, the Russian, a white blur behind the perspex, fighting back. They roared lower and lower. In the rear-view mirror, de la Mazière caught a frightening glimpse of the second Yak chasing him.

'Give the whoreson some lead, damn you, corporal! Feed her fire—*in Heaven's name!*'

'*Jawohl!*' The corporal swung his machine-gun, fired a wild burst at the other Yak. Tracer cut the air in a lethal morse and the Yak broke to the right, leaving the red bullets to hiss by like a swarm of fiery red hornets. The kid had done the trick. De la Mazière took his eyes off the rear-view mirror and concentrated on his victim. He had a few minutes before the second Yak came into the attack once more.

Now the first Russian had pulled out of his spin. Aware that the Stuka was on his tail, coming in for the kill, he started to throw the little fighter all over the place, trying to shake off de la Mazière so that he could gain the advantage of height. De la Mazière hung on grimly. Now the Yak drifted into his gun sight. The German didn't hesitate. He jabbed the button—once, twice, three times. Quick, efficient, sharp, controlled bursts, conserving his ammunition. In vain the Russian twisted and turned, before pushing his stick forward and roaring all out, trying to outdistance de la Mazière. In vain! The German kept after him. Again de la Mazière tapped his firing button. The Stuka trembled and the cockpit flooded with gunsmoke.

A vicious ripple of harsh red flashes ran the length of the Yak. Chunks of gleaming metal flew off. The fighter vibrated madly. The end was near. De la Mazière, teeth gritted painfully, fired again. Behind him his corporal made a sound halfway between a groan and a scream. De la Mazière paid no attention. His whole being was concentrated on the kill.

Abruptly the Yak's prop ceased. White fumes shot from the crippled engine, and an explosion racked the little fighter. Then another. De la Mazière eased his finger from the firing button, still racing after the Yak at 400 kilometres an hour, eyes watchful like those of a hawk, face set in harsh anticipation.

The Yak flipped on its side. With the pilot perhaps dead or wounded and unconscious, it fell screaming out of the sky. Hurtling towards the ground in that last tremendous dive, it vanished into the clouds in the same instant that the second Yak raked the Stuka with a long burst of tracer.

The plane shook under that tremendous impact. De la Mazière could feel the cold air rushing in through a hundred holes, the controls nearly jerked out of his hands by the sledgehammer blows.

Immediately he forgot the 'kill'. The controls started to judder. He flashed an urgent look at his petrol gauge. *Nothing!*

Already he could feel his plane losing power. He flashed another glance at the rear-view mirror. The Yak was making a tight turn, preparing for another run-in. The cloud cover was less than 500 metres away. Could he make it?

He made a lightning decision. If he could escape the Yak,

he'd have to chance that the Ivans had not yet occupied Tazinskaya Field. It was only a few kilometres away. If he had the gas to get up there. . . .

He let the thoughts flash through his mind, automatically going through the routine procedures, as the Yak came barrelling in, guns already blazing, the pilot knowing that if he didn't knock the damned Fritz out of the sky on this run, he could escape into the clouds.

De la Mazière became aware that the corporal wasn't answering the Ivan's fire. Perhaps he was too scared. He mumbled a swift prayer that the rest of the survivors had escaped to Morosovskaya Field, and forced the crippled plane towards the blessed safety of the clouds, the engine coughing and spluttering, as if it might pack up at any second. The Yak was right on his tail. . . .

CHAPTER 3

SOON IT would be dark. Already the black shadows of the night were sliding in sinister silence across the field, past the crashed Stuka, still smouldering and wrapped in bubbling foam, on across the cratered runway, approaching the little group of men, frozen as if for eternity, gazes raised to the empty sky.

The survivors of the 1st SS Stuka Group had returned, not in battle formation but in a straggling line, like geese after a shotgun volley. Everywhere flares had summoned help, arching a fiery red into the grey, lowering sky, and the ambulances, horns sounding an urgent warning, and the fire-trucks had gone out to meet them, bouncing wildly across the bombed field as the Stukas had slammed to the deck in a wild slither of black goo.

Baron Karst, his face a mask of sweat and grime, his grey overalls stinking of explosive and castor oil, had reported with his usual stiff SS formality, bowing from the waist like a caricature of an Imperial Prussian officer as he had saluted. Then, his eagerness all too obvious, he had asked about his fellow group commanders, de la Mazière and von Heiter.

Sombrely, not taking his sad gaze from the sky, Colonel Greim had told him the news. They had still not returned from the mission.

Baron Karst had mumbled the expected expressions of regret, but he had been unable to conceal his joy—and naked ambition. As senior pilot, Greim would be forced to promote him, in spite of what had happened in the past.* He had strode back to his billet, past the ground crew dragging in the

*See *Hawks of Death* for further details

dead body of one of the gunners, whose head had been shot off, his own shoulders erect, his step jaunty. Later, someone would say he had been humming a marching song as he had passed.

Ten minutes later another black speck had appeared on the horizon, trailing thick smoke. Again the alarm bells had jingled and the harassed ground crews had sprung into action as the ambulances and fire-trucks had gone racing out to meet the survivor.

The Stuka had hit the tarmac, bounced six metres in the air, and come crashing down once more with a jarring thud, snapping off its undercarriage. Instantly it had been surrounded by the ground staff.

'*For shit's sake, give him air!*' '*Keep him shitting warm!*', were the cries, as they had carried away the teenage gunner, his blond hair matted with blood, his hand clutching empty air, as if he were trying to hold on to life itself, his eyes rolled back a fish-white.

The pilot had waited till the gesticulating mob had carried off their dying burden, before limping over to Greim. It had been vom Osten, a veteran of 'Forty. He had saluted casually, aimed his thumb at his mouth in the gesture of needing a drink, had gratefully accepted a slug from Greim's silver flask and had shaken his head. 'I'm the shitting last, sir!' he had said with an air of finality. Then he had gone limping off to his quarters, dripping blood on the patches of dirty snow.

That had been half an hour ago. Now the rest of the onlookers had drifted away. With the shadows had come the night cold. An icy wind was beginning to race across the deserted field, straight from Siberia, and over at the mess they were starting to sing. Still the three of them waited, standing there on the tarmac like three statues, gaze fixed on the darkening sky, ears filled with the muted thunder of the heavy guns to the east, the ever-present background music of war.

Colonel Greim, his scarred face expressionless, wept inside. His spirit had collapsed like a dishrag at vom Osten's words. He knew they were true. The veteran wasn't given to making the false claims and boasts of the younger pilots. He *was* the last! Two-thirds of the Group had been lost this day. He could feel the tears drip inside his throat as from an abscess. Veteran and greenbeak alike, they had all been swallowed up in the greedy maws of the God of War.

'It isn't shittingly well fair!' Sergeant Schmidt exploded, his face still black and stained with oil smears, breaking the heavy silence. 'They shouldn't have got Hannemann, the Popov pigs!' He looked up at Greim, his tough old face contorted with emotion, tears in his red-rimmed eyes. 'They can't have got him, sir, *can they?*'

Numbly Greim shook his head. What could he say? Why should it have been Hannemann, Schmidt's old running mate since the Condor Legion? Why should it have been de la Mazière, Hanno von Heiter, any of them for that matter? *Why?* But there was no answer to that great, unanswerable question asked by all fighting men at one time or other.

'Papa' Diercks, the white-haired senior crew chief who, it was rumoured, had served as crew chief for the great Richthofen himself in the Old War, laid his hand gently on Greim's. 'Sir,' he said softly, 'forgive me. But I think it's no use waiting any longer. They say the kitchen bulls are serving thick pea soup and sausage tonight, *real* sausage, not ersatz.' He smiled sadly, his face already vanishing in the night shadows.

'Are you concerned about fart-soup at a time like—' Slack Arse Schmidt began, enraged, but Papa Diercks silenced him with an upraised hand.

'Ease it, Slack Arse,' he said. 'No use, blowing yer stack. . . . They're not coming back, *never!*' Wordlessly they turned and started to walk slowly to the sound of the drunken singing, shoulders bent in defeat like three old men. Behind them the field lay silent, the sky to the east empty of all life, save for the noiseless, pink flickering of the permanent barrage.

Hanno von Heiter flung an anxious glance at the Stuka's temperature gauge. It was rising alarmingly at the same time as his oil pressure was sliding through the floor. They were in trouble, serious trouble! Even Fifi sensed it. She lay silently, as if she did not want to draw the slightest attention to her furry person. Von Heiter patted her lovingly and snapped, 'Hannemann, all clear to the rear?'

'Not even the smell of an Ivan, sir,' Hannemann answered promptly. 'The only stink is gas,' he added, his voice falling.

'Just as I expected,' von Heiter answered, relieved that they had shaken off their pursuers. 'I think we've been holed in the gas tank and probably hit in the engine as well. We're losing oil pressure at a hell of a rate.' He glanced at the needle. It was motionless. It could go no farther. In a few minutes, the big Juno engine might well seize up.

'What's the drill, sir?'

'Well, I don't fancy baling out for one,' the pilot answered, casting a look at the dark earth sliding below, his own shadow, gigantically distorted, racing across the endless fir forest. 'You could be lost for ever and a day down there before anyone found you.'

'There's wolves and bears, too,' Hannemann agreed.

'Shut up!' von Heiter snapped, his fear rising abruptly. 'You'd knock the shitting heart out of anyone, Hannemann!'

'Just being helpful, sir,' Hannemann replied without rancour.

'Well, turn your helpfulness to spotting a suitable landing ground,' von Heiter cried, as the engine gave a thick throaty cough, stopped for one alarming moment, and then broke into full life. 'There isn't much time left, Hannemann.'

'Sir!'

They concentrated, straining their eyes against the

growing darkness, as the plane came lower and lower, searching for a fire-break, or some straight piece of cart-track. But there was nothing, just the limitless, dark-green carpet of the firs.

Von Heiter lowered his seat to protect his head and neck in case the plane turned turtle if they crashed. Behind him Hannemann did the same and slid back the hood to allow the icy cold air to stream in. He was not going to take the chance of being trapped inside the cockpit. All the time the Stuka was coming down steadily, angry blue sparks erupting from the engine. Any moment now she would either go up in flames as the leaking gas ignited, or the engine would stop and they would go into their final dive. Desperately the two of them searched that alien terrain for somewhere to land before it was too late.

The engine stopped. The Stuka's nose dropped. Sweat streamed down von Heiter's back in hot rivulets in spite of the icy air; his undershirt stuck to him like a clammy, cold towel. It could only be a matter of seconds now. 'Prepare to ba—'

'Sir!' Hannemann's excited shout broke into his command to jump. 'Look to port!'

Von Heiter swung his head round. A faint white streak cut through the green gloom. *Could it be?*

Hannemann seemed to read his thoughts. 'It *is*, sir. I'll bet my last cent on it. *It's Tazinskaya Field!*'

'But the Old Man said the Ivans were heading for it,' von Heiter objected, fighting to keep the crippled plane airborne. 'He warned us off. Remember?'

'I know, sir. But what else can we do? Perhaps the Ivans haven't reached it yet. I've seen no sign of them so far. Hell, that place down there looks as if nobody's been there since the year dot. Besides—' He strained his eyes, face contorted as the wind buffeted it. 'I swear there's one of our crates down there—at three o'clock, if you can see it, sir.'

Von Heiter narrowed his eyes. 'God in heaven, Hannemann,' he exclaimed, 'you're right, and by the way the firs are bending back its prop is still turning! That's prop-wash for sure and that means—'

'One of our lot is down there and the Ivans haven't arrived yet!' Hannemann beat him to it in an exuberant roar. 'So what are we waiting for, sir? Let's go before this crate runs out on us!'

'Yes indeed!' von Heiter chortled, hope surging through his body.

At his side, Fifi, his absurd pooch, began to yelp excitedly, as if she, too, sensed a chance after all.

They hit the cratered runway with a thump that jarred von Heiter's teeth. One tyre burst immediately, like an 88mm shell exploding, stopping the Stuka's mad dash across the tarmac, the sound of metal being torn to shreds almost impossible to bear. It stopped just short of the other Stuka parked there, its own engine still turning.

Von Heiter was flung forward, the harness cutting cruelly into his shoulders. Something punched him in the jaw. He yelped, and beside him Fifi buried herself deeper into his side, whimpering. Behind, Hannemann cursed as his head slapped against the cockpit and blood spurted from his forehead. The Stuka stood on its nose for a moment before, slowly, it fell on its belly, the dust rising up in a swift cloud and blinding the dazed men.

They sat, limp and drained, the dust settling around them, the only sound that of the wind in the trees, the softly turning engine of the other Stuka, and the drip-drip of escaping fluid.

Hannemann shook his head. With a hand that trembled, he wiped the cold sweat and blood from his brow and raised himself from the shattered plane to survey the other Stuka, its engine still ticking over and a white blur visible in the rear of its cockpit. It had to be the air-gunner, he told himself; but why didn't the shitheel do anything? At least, he could turn and look at them. It wasn't every day that someone made a landing like they had.

'Hannemann,' von Heiter said slowly, his voice uncertain, puzzled, 'that's Major de la Mazière's plane. I recognise the markings.'

'Yessir,' Hannemann answered, his tough Berlin voice not altogether steady. 'I thought it was. But why . . . why is his engine still running and why doesn't that arse-with-ears over there notice we're here? What's up with him? Is he getting in some Z's or something?'

Von Heiter frowned and raised himself slowly in the cockpit, cuddling the whimpering Fifi to his chest. He stared at the dark outline of the Stuka in the gathering gloom. 'And where's Major de la Mazière?'

'Here!'

The two of them swung round electrically and even Hannemann felt the small hairs at the back of his neck grow erect with the eeriness of the confrontation.

Ten metres away, de la Mazière stood with his feet apart like a grey ghost, a sub-machine cradled across his chest, handsome face hollowed out to a dark death's head.

Instinctively, that old familiar sinking feeling told von Heiter that something was wrong, seriously wrong. 'Are the Ivans here?' he whispered.

'They were,' de la Mazière answered, still motionless. 'But they've gone . . . for a while.'

Hannemann dropped over the side into the mess of stones and broken metal and crunched across to the other Stuka. In the poor light, he could see that the rear of the canopy had been shattered by machine-gun fire. Where the gunner's skull should have been, there was a gory red hole. The drip-dripping sound came from his escaping blood.

'He's dead. They're all dead.' De la Mazière's voice was harsh and angry. 'Every last one of them! Even the Russian women. Slaughtered without mercy.'

Von Heiter gave a strange keening sound and Hannemann

exclaimed. 'But why the women, sir?' He meant the Russian women *hiwis*,* who worked in the kitchens and messes and were not above letting them down for some eager, randy noncom if the price were right. 'They were only servants. . . .'

De la Mazière shrugged. 'They worked for us, didn't they, sergeant?' he countered. 'That's sufficient reason for them. Come—see!' He beckoned before striding off to the little cluster of tin-roofed wooden huts which had been their 'home' for the last three months. Unwillingly von Heiter and Hannemann followed. Behind them the night shadows stole in from the dark secret woods and abruptly, it seemed to a suddenly terrified von Heiter, he could hear strange, suspicious sounds coming on all sides from the woods. He hurried after an angry, long-legged de la Mazière, clutching Fifi to his chest.

'They took their pleasure first,' de la Mazière snapped and indicated the door opening into the gloom of the hut that smelled of woman and black Russian tobacco. 'Of course. Then they did this.' He stepped back and stretched out a hand as if he were a head waiter indicating that an honoured guest should enter.

Von Heiter looked inside and reeled back, hot vomit flooding his mouth, Fifi dropped in his shock. Hannemann pushed back his flying helmet in his tough Berlin manner, preparing himself for the sight. Senior noncoms were never shocked, not in public, at least.

'Oh, my God,' he whispered in a hushed voice as he saw what had happened. '*Oh my sweet shitting God!*' He thrust his fist into his mouth to prevent himself being sick on the spot. He had seen plenty of terrible things in this war, and in Spain, but never anything like this. 'But they've cut their tits off, sir!' he stammered, pushing his hands out in front of him, as if to

*German Army slang for the million-strong army of Russians who worked—and fought—for Germany in WWII

ward off that terrible sight, 'and they've done things to—'
he swallowed—'to their lower bodies with bayonets or
something!' Again he fought back the hot sickening green bile
that threatened to choke him.

'There's worse back there,' said de la Mazière, jerking a
thumb towards the messhall complex. 'You remember that
old Pope?'

Hannemann nodded. The Russian orthodox priest in his
greasy black robes, high hat and long flowing beard, had
appeared out of nowhere a couple of months ago and in a kind
of dumbshow had asked to bless their Stukas before they had
set off on their missions. Karst had had him thrown off the
field. He hated 'men of God'. But the old Russian 'Pope' had
reappeared and in the end he had been accepted. Some of the
pilots regarded him as a kind of mascot, and wouldn't take off
without a blessing from him. In return, he had been allowed
to sleep on the base and been given leftovers from the
kitchens. A harmless Popov idiot, Hannemann had always
thought him, who had always smiled benignly when the men
had made violent masturbating gestures to indicate that was
how he spent his time when he wasn't blessing the departing
planes.

'First they nailed him to the cookhouse door by his greasy
beard,' de la Mazière said grimly, eyes now searching the
surrounding woods, as if he expected something—or some-
body—to emerge. 'Then they ripped off his clothes and
crucified him there like Jesus. That wasn't all. They nailed up
two of our fellows, to his left and right—they must have been
left behind when the rest fled, the poor shits.'

'Like the two thieves, 'Hannemann whispered, remembering his pre-confirmation Bible classes. 'Oh, my God!'

'Exactly. But don't ask me what they did with the old
Pope's own crucifix.'

At last Hanno von Heiter recovered his voice. 'Detlev,' he
cried fearfully, eyes flashing to left and right wildly, 'let's get
out of here while there's still time.' He gulped feverishly.

'Don't let's waste time jawing here. They could come back at any time, the murdering swine!'

Detlev de la Mazière shook his head slowly, his harsh features determined in the poor light. 'No, Hanno, I don't think they'll be back so soon. My guess is that they are partisans, not regular Red Army units. The swine are using the push to the Dnieper to carry out their usual barbaric looting and killing. Hell, they're no better than the wolves of the forest. Once the steam has gone out of the Red Army attack they'll slink back to their lairs to enjoy their prey. We've still got time.'

Hanno von Heiter contained his fear with a visible effort, hugging his little dog to his chest like a mother might a child, afraid that it would be dragged from her the very next moment. 'But they'll hear the noise of your engine, Detlev,' he objected, chest heaving. 'Sound carries for kilometres at this time of the day, especially in the middle of nowhere, like this place.'

'I suppose they will.'

Hanno grasped his comrade's arm. 'Then in God's name, let's get in your plane and fly off while we've still got time, Detlev!'

De la Mazière favoured von Heiter with an icy smile. 'That's just the trouble, my dear Hanno. My plane *won't* fly!'

Von Heiter moaned and his shoulders sagged. For one awful moment, Hannemann thought he might burst into tears. Swiftly, he said, 'But why keep the prop going then, sir?'

'Because I have a plan, you big rogue. I had just filled her up with all the gas I could find when you came in to make an absolutely dreadful landing which, apart from destroying your crate, did the same thing to my hopes of escaping with you. So there had to be an alternative.'

'What, sir?' Hannemann was puzzled.

From the surrounding forests, the firs beginning to rustle now in the icy evening breeze, there came a faint hooting sound. Hannemann felt a cold finger of fear trace its way down his spine. It could be wood-owls, but it could also be the kind of animal noise the partisans used to signal to each other.

De la Mazière's strange icy lethargy, caused by the sights he had just experienced, was replaced by a burst of sudden electric energy; he had heard, too. 'I reckon we could be ten or twelve kilometres from Marienpol. You remember the place?'

Hannemann nodded. It was the nearest village to the field, linked with a rough track through the woods, broad enough for a couple of trucks.

'My guess is—my *hope* is—that Marienpol is still in German hands. We are going to reach it this night and report what we have seen here. One day there is going to be a reckoning. Someone is going to pay for this.' He extended his hand to include the whole of that sad silent place and its massacred civilians and airmen. 'If it's the last thing I do.'

'But the plane can't fly, sir!' Hannemann protested.

'I know, you big, thick-headed horned ox. But it can *move*, can't it?'

Hannemann's eyes lit up. 'You mean *along the road*, sir?' He chortled with sudden hope.

'Of course. Haven't we landed and taken off from country roads time and time again in the old days. Hannemann? Remember France, Greece, Crete?'

Hannemann's happy look vanished. 'But, sir, that was in day-time, with good light, and there were no shitting Popov partisans to play nasty tricks on us.'

'So? What do you think you joined the service for? Suds and shit-on-shingle for breakfast, every shitting day!'* He grinned at Hannemann. 'Rather tough shit on you if you did, Hannemann. Now you're really going to earn yer pay, arse-with-plush-ears!'

The enthusiastic coarseness made Hannemann's doubts

*Beer and chipped beef on bread

vanish immediately. If anyone could pull it off, it would be the Major. 'What are we waiting for, sir?'

'What, indeed? Over there we've got our own kind of tank, the new Stuka land-cruiser, armed with three 7.62mms and one—' Hastily he unslung his machine pistol and tossed it carelessly to a numb von Heiter, 'popgun. Come on, the two of you—and that stupid pooch of yours, too, Hanno—let's get aboard!'

As if the devil himself were behind them, they started to run for the waiting 'Stuka land-cruiser'.

CHAPTER 4

'*Herr Oberst! Herr Oberst!*'

The urgent voice seemed to come from far, far away, cutting into his confused dream of burning planes and horribly mutilated men. Somewhere a long way off, he thought he could hear engines being warmed up.

'*Herr Oberst, wachen Sie bitte auf! Es ist sehr wichtig. Bitte, Herr Oberst!*'

Greim groaned and refused to open his eyes, as the hand shook his shoulder. 'Go away,' he moaned, 'go away till next year.'

'But sir, it's top priority. *Straight from the Führer's Supreme Headquarters, sir!*' Greim, still drunk with sleep, had the impression that whoever was trying to wake him had snapped to attention at the mention of the Führer.

'Tell me in the morning then,' he said through lips sticky with sleep.

'But it's an immediate, sir,' the unknown voice persisted. 'Please wake up and read it. I've already entered it in the duty roster. I'm responsible. They'll have me in Torgau* if I don't deliver it to you now, sir. *Please!*'

Reluctantly, recognising the note of pleading in the other man's voice, Greim opened his eyes. The blackout curtains had already been drawn but he could dimly see the blood-red ball of the sun beginning to edge its way over the horizon. On the field, mechanics were busy around his Messerschmitt, although he had not given any orders for it to be readied for him at this hour. He stared up at the anxious young duty noncom in his steel helmet, pistol at his hip, two messages in

*A notorious German military prison

his gloved hand. He rubbed the scum from his lips with the back of his hand and indicated his false teeth resting in a glass of water on the chair next to his bed. 'Give me the fangs,' he said thickly. 'I can't think without them in.'

'Yessir.'

Gingerly the NCO dipped his gloved hand into the water and daintily handed the teeth to his C.O.

Greim grinned. 'Don't worry, they won't bite you, laddie,' he said. 'They go with this.' He indicated his scarred face. 'Both went in 'forty when you were still undoubtedly pressing your short pants on a school-bench.'

'Yessir,' the NCO said dutifully and, as if they were red-hot, handed the messages to Greim, glad to be relieved of the documents. Both were stamped in red, *'Geheime Reichssache'*.*

Awkwardly Greim slit one open with his thumb and unfolded the message. Half a dozen 'Priorities' were stamped in black at the top, and no wonder. It was from Colonel-General Jodl, the Führer's Chief-of-Staff, and read simply, *'Colonel Greim, 1st SS Stuka Group, to report to FHQ** immediately, stop. Prepare to brief Führer on Ju 87–GI at twelve hundred hours, stop. Specifically, employment against enemy armoured vehicles. Stop. Acknowledge receipt. Stop. Jodl.'*

Greim whistled softly through his false teeth and the noncom said hastily, 'Air Fleet Four HQ already informed us by phone to have your plane ready and fuelled by zero six hundred, sir! There's nigger sweat and a bowl of giddi-up soup*** on the way from the cookhouse, sir.'

'Good man,' Greim murmured and ripped open the other message, wondering what all this was about. He had not been summoned to meet the Führer since the great days of 1940 when everybody thought the Stuka was a war-winning weapon—'the Führer's own flying artillery'—and Stuka pilots

*The equivalent of 'top secret'
**Führer HQ
***Black coffee and goulash

were the darlings of the poison-dwarf* and his propaganda machine. Now in this year of 1943, three years later, the Top Brass in Berlin had almost forgotten the Stuka's existence.

Greim whistled again. It was a morning of surprises, that was for sure. The second message was from Goering's Chief-of-Staff, General Jeschonnek, and it was just as mysterious as the other.

'*1st SS Stuka Group will report to Rechlin Field forthwith. As of receipt of this message, it is to be withdrawn from operations. Its aircraft will remain behind to be taken over by Sixth Reserve Stuka Group. Second Battalion, Fourth Luftwaffe Field Division will take over guard duties immediately.*'

As if on cue, Greim was suddenly aware of heavy motors labouring through the black mud on the road which led to the Field and, by raising himself on one elbow, could just see the first of the open trucks, packed with soldiers in the field-grey of the *Luftwaffe* infantry, turning in at the gate to be stared at by the amazed sentries.

'*Du grosser Gott!*' he cursed, bewildered, as he swung himself out of bed, 'What in three devils' name is going on?'

It was a question that the puzzled officers and men of the 1st SS Stuka Group, who had survived the slaughter of the Dnieper, were asking themselves, too, as they crowded around the troop train, preparing, each in his own way, for the three-day trip back to the Reich, while Red Cross sisters in their striped uniforms were busy ladling out coffee and soup from steaming kettles. There weren't many takers, however, for most of the men—and some of the elegant black-clad officers, too—were happily drunk by now on black market potato vodka and strong Russian beer bought from the ragged, fur-hatted dealers hawking their wares from huge enamel, foaming pails.

*Nickname for Dr Goebbels, the Minister of Propaganda

'*Rechlin*,' they said thickly, 'but that's the Luftwaffe's experimental field! What the hell should hairy-assed old hares like us be doing there? They don't experiment on cannonfodder such as us, comrades, do they?'

'*We're being relieved—on account of old age!*' they chortled, faces happy and flushed with beer and vodka. 'Hell, some of us old heads have been out here so long, we don't even speak German any more. *Ponemayu?*'

'*They're gonna turn us into shitting stubble-hoppers!*' some said warily, indicating the troop-train steaming in from the Reich, packed with innocent-faced fresh infantry bound for the Dnieper front, staring at the crowd of drunken shouting airmen, caps at the back of their heads and tunics ripped open, as if they came from another world. 'Mark my words. That's what it's all about. The shitting old Stuka has had its day. They'll give us a sniff of the old woman's gash back home, two weeks of square-bashing, issue us with the shitting ole "08"* and it's back to the front and the shitting meat-grinder, mates.'

'*What does it shitting matter? Up the cups, comrades, the night'll be cold!* Who wants to live for ever, anyhow? We're going home to mother, comrades. We'll dance the mattress polka with the missus! We'll soak our tonsils in suds from morning till night! We'll stuff our guts with sausage and sauerkraut! We'll shit on a real shitter instead o' them old thunderboxes. We'll get rid o' the little bees.** *We're going shitting well home! HURRAH!*'

A few were morose in spite of the vodka, the beer, the prospect of leave in the Reich. They had lost too many comrades in the limitless Russian wastes, buried in some god-forsaken spot on the steppe, a place without even a name.

Slack Arse Schmidt was one such, as he squatted morosely in the corner of the senior noncoms' compartment, nursing his metal canteen of vodka, huddled on the hard wooden seat

---

*'08' standard infantry rifle
**Soldiers' slang for lice

surrounded by his gear, as old Papa Diercks proudly unpacked the goodies he had brought for the trip.

'One mule dick,' he announced, putting the hard slab of sausage on the bench. 'A tin o' monkey grease.' Margarine followed. 'A packet of putty.' He dropped the soft cheese on the tin of margarine, 'plus the *pièce de résistance*, as the frogs call it, *one whole case of looted lung torpedos*,' he indicated the box of Russian cigars, *and a naughty book to get us in the right frame of mind for mother back home!* He winked knowingly at a sombre-faced Slack Arse. 'What do they say? The second thing a soldier does when he get home with his old woman is—to take off his pack. Ha, ha!' He laughed uproariously at the old joke, and the other senior noncoms joined in happily. 'I'm gonna tell my old woman, once she's loosed down her black silk drawers, now come on, mother, have a good look at the floor—*'cos you're only gonna be seeing the ceiling for the next forty-eight hours! Ha, ha!*'

There was another burst of drunken laughter. But again, Slack Arse did not join in. Instead he squatted miserably, staring at nothing.

'What's up with you, Slack Arse?' someone cried encouragingly. 'You look like the bloke who just discovers he's a warm brother* at the door of a knocking shop laden with free gash!'

'Fuck off,' Slack Arse said morosely. 'Leave me fucking alone, willya?'

Papa Diercks patted him on the shoulder sympathetically. 'Take it easy, old house. It's always been this way. It was the same in the old war, the same in Spain, remember, and it's no different in 1943 neither. Believe you me.'

'But Hannemann,' Slack Arse Schmidt began to protest.

But Diercks didn't give him a chance. He thrust a cigar in the other NCO's mouth and said with false heartiness, 'Get that lung torpedo lit up, Slack Arse, and forget. Who

*Slang for a homosexual

knows—this time next year we might have gone hop too, if we survive that long, comrade. *Prost*, stick this behind yer collar!'

Survival was on Acting Captain Baron Karst's mind, too, as the officious RTO staff ran up and down the platform blowing their whistles, trying to shoo away the begging peasants in their ragged clothes and the hawkers, while the steel-helmeted chaindogs watched hard-eyed and ready to shoot if any of the infantry going up to the front attempted to get out of their troop train. '*Meine Herren*,' he announced, one hundred per cent confident, face full of haughty arrogance, as he gazed around at the excited, young faces of his listeners, 'we are being summoned to great things. We are the survivors, forged in the flame of battle, tempered and as hard as Krupp steel now. The Führer has something in mind for us, believe you me. After all, we are his élite.'

'But what, *Hauptsturm*?' one of his young hearers asked, gazing in admiration at the officer with his chest covered in decorations, the coveted Knight's Cross hanging carelessly from his collar, beneath a lean killer's face they had all known ever since their schooldays. Wasn't he and the rest of the 'old hares' a public hero, after all? 'Why have they taken our kites off us? Where's the Old Man off to? And why are we being sent to an experimental field?' He shook his blond head. 'It's all very confusing, sir.'

'The Führer in his infinite wisdom,' Karst pontificated, relishing being the centre of all eyes as the most senior surviving officer of the 1st SS, 'will tell us all in his own good time, Hans.' He lit a thin cheroot with calculated slowness, letting them hang on his words, while outside the red-capped civilian station-master raised his little metal signal stick, and the steam escaped from the locomotive's boiler in a frantic hiss.

'But one can make an educated guess at what is going on?' He smiled at them thinly. 'Can't one?'

They craned forward eagerly, as von Einem in the corner, his wounded foot propped up in front of him, snorted angrily,

'For God's sake, Karst, piss or get off the stupid pisspot, willya!'

Karst ignored him, though he made a mental note that once they were on ops again, von Einem would get the shittiest of missions. He could rely on that. 'The Führer summons Colonel Greim. One,' he ticked it off on his well-manicured fingers. 'We are sent to the experimental field. Two. Finally, three, we lose our somewhat antiquated planes.'

'*Antiquated!*' von Einem laughed hollowly. 'That's not the word for them. They should have been sunk with the shitting Ark!'

Again Karst ignored the veteran's crude comment. He knew he had the young greenbeaks' undivided attention. 'What does it all add up to?' He answered his own question. 'I shall tell you, *meine Herren*, the balloon is soon to go up again somewhere or other—and we, gentlemen, the élite of the élite are going to be given a very special role in this new op, whatever it may be. Believe me, that is what this surprising move is about. The Führer personally has selected the First SS Stuka Group. He knows he can rely on us, *was?*'

Their eyes blazed with fanatic pride and their faces hardened at the bold declaration. They threw out their skinny chests and dearly wished they were as laden with 'tin' as Karst and von Einem.

In the corner the wounded veteran muttered and buried his nose in a French pornographic magazine.

Karst ignored him. 'Gentlemen, I am not a betting man, but at this moment I would be prepared to wager a case of champus with any one of you that the 1st SS will be on ops again before this spring is out, that I would.' He settled back into his plush seat with a happy knowing smile on his lean arrogant face as the excited talk at his announcement started up around him. His luck had turned again. His rivals were dead and he was alive. He closed his eyes happily and made himself comfortable.

Outside the station-master's whistle shrilled. There was a hiss of steam and a clatter of steel as the wheels tried to grip the cold icy track.

'*Pfui*,' the trapped infantrymen called contemptuously and whistled their disapproval through their teeth. '*Baa . . . baa!*' they mocked the sheep, as the train heading west slowly started to pull away, knowing they were going to their death. 'The captain . . . the captain . . . he's got a hole in his arse,' the Luftwaffe men called back drunkenly. 'Follow me, men, I've got a hole in my arse!'

'*Pfui . . . shitheels . . . piss pansies . . . asparagus Tarzans . . . perverted banana suckers*,' the miserable angry infantrymen yelled, as the train gathered speed. *Five against one . . . five against one.*' They crowded to the open window, making obscene gestures to the laughing Luftwaffe men. 'Watch you don't shittingly well go blind!' The train's speed increased. Now the carriages, filled with yelling angry infantrymen, started to blur. '*Auf wiedersehen—in Moskau, Scheisskerle!*' they cried defiantly, as the Luftwaffe men closed their windows and slumped back on their wooden benches.

'That'll be the day!' came a cynical bellow. 'That'll be the day, comrades!'

Karst closed his eyes, a contented look on his face. He had promised himself he would be a general officer before this war was over. For a while he had suffered some setbacks. Now things were moving forward again. He'd have those general's stars yet.

Now they were rattling out of the little Russian station, the infantry train disappearing into the smoke behind them. They were heading for the Reich. They had done it. They had survived Russia, by God! *They were heading back home!*

A thousand kilometres farther west, alone in his Messer-schmidt, Colonel Greim, too, breathed a fervent sigh of relief as he sighted the first silver sheen of the East Prussian lakes which meant he was approaching Germany. In a matter of minutes he would be leaving that accursed Russia—for a while, at least. He flashed a glance at the vast empty landscape below. What terrible suffering had taken place down there since 22 June, 1941!* What horror! What endless misery! The place was simply too big, too big to conquer even for that vaunted 'Greatest Captain of All Times', Adolf Hitler. The Russian plain surged to every horizon. Whole armies had been swallowed up and vanished without trace down there in these last terrible years.

For a fleeting moment, he had a vision of ghostly battalions toiling noiselessly ever eastwards, the men's strained eyes fixed on an unknown destination, urged on by some awesome destiny until they disappeared beyond the burning horizon, with not even the marks of their footprints to signal their passing.

De la Mazière, Hanno von Heiter, Senior Sergeant Hannemann—and half a hundred other young men he had known, and perhaps even loved for a while, were part of that spectral procession. Now they were gone, lost, vanished, never to be seen again, dead for 'Folk, Fatherland and Führer', as the official formula had it, before they had even begun to live. *Gone!*

His weary old eyes flooded with tears at the memory of their bold, hopeful young faces, as they filed by in his mind, though suddenly their gaze held a look of abrupt accusation, as if somehow *he* were to blame for their ghastly fate; *he* had sent them to their deaths in this accursed country.

Colonel Greim shook his head. That spectral parade vanished and with it the tears. Down below the first neat white-painted East Prussian village flashed into sight. It looked so peaceful, so German, so remote from the horror of the war in Russia. He was back with his own kind. He was home.

*The date of Germany's invasion of Russia

Suddenly overwhelmed by the ecstasy and joy of that knowledge, on sudden impulse he swung the Messerschmidt into a tremendous victory roll, roaring through the bright blue East Prussian sky. It was as if he were a kid of eighteen again, buzzing the field in France in the Old War after having shot down his first 'Tommy'. *He was home!*

PART TWO

The Cannonbird

CHAPTER 1

'*MARIENPOL!*' de la Mazière announced and braked. Wearily he wiped the dust and sweat off his strained face and stared down at the little village, outlined a stark black against the first blood-red rays of the new sun. All night long, with Hanno spelling him at the controls, they had edged their way in the crippled Stuka through the thick forests, each new bend creating a fresh alarm, a sudden electric tingling of the nerves, a thunder of the heart, as they tensed for the dangers it might bring. But there had been none, just an occasional deer startled by the noise and running wildly for cover, and once a great brown bear that stood stupidly upright in the middle of the track for what seemed an age before it, too, had taken fright and had fled, lumbering into the firs. The three of them might well have been alone in this vast green wilderness.

They stared at the cluster of dirty cottages grouped round the onion-towered church that had not been used as a house of worship these thirty-odd years, as if at a mirage. Did Marienpol really exist?

It did and it was clear that it was still occupied, for to the rear of the village a thin wisp of blue smoke was drifting lazily into the dawn sky.

'What do you think, sir?' Hannemann asked from the back, while Hanno von Heiter cradled the whimpering poodle to his chest.

De la Mazière frowned. 'Don't rightly know, Hannemann,' he answered slowly, surveying the place with a trained eye, swinging from left to right systematically, and wishing that he possessed a pair of binoculars. 'If I recollect, the place used to be garrisoned by a golden pheasant from the SA and half a dozen *Hiwis*?'

'That's right, sir,' Hannemann agreed. 'A proper old fart

cannon from the Berlin SA. Spent most of the time supping *pivo* and knocking off the local *matkas** while the *Hiwis* watched for the partisans. Typical golden pheasant.'**

'Sometimes I think you're a damned commie yourself, Hannemann,' de la Mazière said mildly, not taking his gaze off the silent, *too silent*, village. 'Talking about our glorious Party officials like that!'

'I've shat better turds,' Hannemann said unabashed. 'But where is the fat-arsed pig now, that's the question?'

'Exactly.'

'Do you think *they* . . . are down there?' Hanno faltered, clutching the poodle even tighter.

De la Mazière shrugged. 'Could be, Hanno. It would be a likely place for them to head to before they disappear back into the forest again. And I'm sure that the fat golden pheasant and his *Hiwis* wouldn't be able to stop them for long.'

'But what are we going to do, Detlev?' Hanno quavered.

'What can we do?' De la Mazière shrugged again. 'If we want to stay with these wheels,' he indicated the Stuka, 'a little longer we've got to go through the village. There is no other way, you know.'

'If you ask me, sir, which you won't,' Hannemann chimed in, 'I'm all for sticking with the wheels. I had enough of hoofing it to last me a lifetime when I did my basic training back in thirty-six.'

He beamed at the Major and Major de la Mazière beamed back. For all his hearty dislike of the officer class and SS officers, in particular, Hannemann was a good person to have about in a tight situation.

'Wheels it is then,' he said. 'Hanno, you take over the stick.' He grabbed their machine pistol, their only useful handfire weapon for other than very close range. 'I'm off on the port

---

*Russian for 'beer' and 'mothers'
**Contemptuous name for Nazi Party officials on account of their love of gold braid

wing. Hannemann, you cover both flanks with your popgun. *Klar?*'

'*Klar!*' Hannemann rapped, face hard and alert.

'All right, Hanno. Chocs away. Here we go!'

The engine started up with a furious roar once more and de la Mazière flashed a quick look at the village below to see if it had alerted anyone. Nothing moved. There was not even the sudden bark of a hound or the startled squawking of the villagers' chickens. Nothing. The place might well have been completely abandoned, save for the fact that that lone chimney smoked on. Swiftly de la Mazière clambered out of the cockpit as Hanno began to edge the crippled plane down the incline, and slithered on to the port wing, machine pistol at the ready, feet braced against the jagged flak hole to keep himself in place. If Marienpol was held by the partisans, he wanted to be prepared for the fireworks to come.

Metre by metre, his face strained and glazed with sweat, as if it had been greased with Vaseline, Hanno edged the Stuka down the tricky incline, its wheels buried in a splutter of black mud and pebbles, the young aristocrat praying that it wouldn't skid or bog down. Then they really would be sitting ducks out here in the open. Next to him, Fifi bowed her shaggy head and hid her eyes with her paws, as if she already knew that there was trouble to come and wanted no part of it. Behind Hanno, Hannemann drew back his bolt with metallic finality and tensed. Suddenly the very air was heavy with thick tension.

De la Mazière clicked off his safety, his nostrils assailed by a strange scorched smell, which he could not identify, coming from the village below. Had the Popov villagers killed a pig and, as was their custom, scorched off the bristle with burning pitch brands? He dismissed the smell and concentrated on the task in hand, as the Stuka came ever closer.

He could see the first houses quite clearly. White-washed, turf-roofed affairs, with the yellowed tobacco leaves from the previous autumn still drying and curing under the eaves, the gardens surrounded by tumbledown picket fences. Nothing different from a hundred other miserable villages he had encountered in these last years in the 'Peasants' and Workers' Paradise': the sort of place that hadn't been seen in rural Germany since the Middle Ages. Still there was no sign of the inhabitants and why hadn't the skinny-ribbed, half-starved hounds that usually ran wild in such places begun their customary howling and barking? Had the whole population run away?

Hanno fought the Stuka round a slight bend, slithering and sliding all the time, the mud flying up about the under-carriage, the prop whirling madly, as he gave the engine extra power.

De la Mazière told himself, if there were anybody in the damned, tumbledown place, they must be shitting deaf if they didn't hear the racket they were making! He realised that his hands were wet with sweat in spite of the dawn cold and he knew why—he was scared.

'Sir!' Hannemann's voice rose above the roar of the engine.

'What?' he called back, clinging on grimly, eyes fixed on his front.

'The big pole—the maypole or whatever it is, sir. *Look!*'

De la Mazière shot a swift glance to his left. He gasped at what he saw hanging there. Now he knew what the smell was. It was not a pig that was hanging there. It was a human being!

There hung a 'golden pheasant', stripped of his gold-braided SA finery, his swollen body naked and charred coal-black in parts, the flesh split here and there, a thick fig-red juice oozing from the wounds. A light brown smoke still wreathed the scorched head, as the golden pheasant, suspended by his heels, gently rotated in the breeze, as if on a spit.

'OH, my God!' Hanno retched and almost lost control of the plane, 'What . . . *whoooo?*' The startled cry seemed to go on for ever, as the first angry flame stabbed the blue air, and suddenly, a black object was hurtling towards them, trailing fiery angry sparks.

'*Panzerfaust!*'* de la Mazière snapped and, without aiming, fired a wild burst from his little m.p. at the first tumbledown *isba.***

The rocket hissed by them and exploded in a mad rush of fire, flame and steel ten metres away. The Stuka rocked crazily under the impact. Hanno fought to hold it on the muddy track.

Now Hannemann's machine-gun joined in the frenetic chatter of de la Mazière's m.p. as, on all sides, firing erupted and the first angry slugs began to rip the length of the land-bound plane.

'Hit the shitting tube!' de la Mazière cried and aimed a rapid burst at a couple of ragged partisans attempting to rush from a doorway to the left. They crumpled like broken dolls. Another flashed from a garden, hand raised, poised to throw a stick-grenade. Hannemann's burst ripped him in half. The grenade tumbled to the ground and exploded, wreathing him in smoke and flame. A moment later all that was left of the partisan was a jumbled mess of gory flesh hanging from the nearest tree like a collection of grisly human fruit.

The sweat pouring down his face, Fifi barking crazily at his side, Hanno 'hit the tube'. The engine roared, its echo reverberating madly, as they entered the confines of the village, the air stabbed with flame and flecked with black puffballs of explosions.

From high above on the church, a group of partisans fumbled with a captured heavy machine gun.

Hannemann didn't give them a chance. '*Eat this, Popov shit-eaters!*' he snarled, face contorted with crimson, unreasoning hatred, and pressed the trigger.

*German rocket-launcher
**Russian for 'hut'

The partisans flew apart. They slammed to the ground like bags of wet cement and lay still.

The Stuka rolled on. Its sides were ripped and shredded by bullets, the metal gleaming like silver scars beneath the fabric. Hanging on, as slugs cut the air just above him, de la Mazière wondered just how the plane could stand the punishment. He prayed it would last at least until they were through the village.

He loosed off quick bursts to left and right, watching his bullets howl off the stone walls of the cottages, while behind him, Hannemann, swearing furiously and manning the heavy machine-gun, hosed their immediate front.

A dark object came flying out of one of the windows. De la Mazière recognised it in the same instant that it dropped right in their path in the centre of the muddy village street. It was a massed packet of hand grenades. '*Satchel charge!*' he shrieked above the bitter snap-and-crackle of small arms fire. 'For God's sake—'

Hanno swerved in the very same moment that he yelled. The Stuka's torn wing slammed into one of the houses. It snapped clean off with a sickening, rending sound. For one long agonising second, de la Mazière thought their under-carriage was going to go, to leave them stranded in full view of the ambushers. But the Stuka was tougher than he had thought. Minus one wing like some huge metallic bettle, it careened on through the village, Hanno von Heiter fighting to keep the crippled plane on a straight course. Now the far end of the place started to come into view. They were going to do it!

A youth, who didn't look a day over fourteen, sprang up from behind a pile of logs and hurtled towards the Stuka. De la Mazière fired a swift burst—and missed! Hanging on for dear life, he changed the empty magazine of his m.p. as the youth raised his stick grenade, preparing to throw.

Hannemann beat him to it. He ripped off a tremendous burst. The front of the boy's shirt disappeared in a welter of bloody gore, what looked like red buttonholes stitched the length of his chest. He started to crumple to the ground, legs giving way beneath him. The grenade tumbled from his nerveless fingers and exploded in a vicious purple ball of flame. It blew the kid's head off and it sailed through the air, to roll away into the gutter like an abandoned football.

The edge of the village was only metres away and already the fire was beginning to slacken, as if the partisans had realised that this strange apparition rolling through their midst was going to escape and had lost heart. De la Mazière felt his hopes beginning to rise. He slapped home his last magazine and yelled above the roar of the engine, 'Get ready to bale out once we're in the forest beyond, Hanno . . . and you, too, Hannemann!'

'Sir!' Hannemann cried, raising himself in the cockpit in full view of the enemy, obviously confident, too, that they were going to escape the ambush. 'Ready to go when you do!' He spat contemptuously over the side of the bucking plane. 'What a bunch of currant-crappers they are! Couldn't fight their way out of a shitting—' The words died on his lips.

To their immediate right, a small group of fur-hatted men, rifles slung across their shoulders, were pouring looted gasoline out of jerricans on to the road. It was flooding across the path, filling the dawn air with its cloying sickening stench.

De la Mazière guessed what they were attempting to do. He raised his m.p. and pressed the trigger. Nothing happened! *'Holy strawsack!'* he cursed, beside himself with exasperation and fear, *'not now!'* He tried again. Nothing but a dry click. He had a stoppage!

Hannemann swung his machine gun round to scythe them down. Too late. They ducked for cover. A spluttering, white-sparking object came hurtling into the middle of the road.

'Thermite grenade!' de la Mazière screamed, knowing what was to come.

It erupted in a flurry of spluttering white sparks. A violent, incandescent, blinding glow. A muffled explosion. A whoosh and a horrifying gasp like some fire-spewing primeval monster drawing breath. In a flash the whole road to their front was blazing. A sheet of livid-orange, oil-tinged flame came rushing towards them.

There was no escaping it. The Stuka rolled straight into the holocaust, and was swamped by the flames. The undercarriage gave at once, and the plane collapsed right into the flames, the bullet-rent paintwork bubbling and sizzling under that enormous heat. De la Mazière flung himself off the wing, his uniform already smouldering, and ran panic-stricken through the flames, the greedy little tongue of fire licking at his running feet, nostrils full of the stench of burning.

Gasping for breath, hands held in front of their faces to protect them from the searing heat, the other two followed, Fifi yelping hysterically. Behind them the flames leapt higher and higher, crawling up the wrecked plane. All the same, the intensity of the fire kept their ambushers at bay—for a while. For even as they pelted out of the fire, de la Mazière knew they would be waiting there in safety to mow them down mercilessly, once they broke free.

But that wasn't to be. In the very same moment that he burst out of the flames, his uniform smouldering and holed with burns, the Stuka's gas tank exploded, and the flames slopped down to the side of the street where the partisans were waiting. In a flash, the partisans were aflame too, turned into human torches, the fire swamping them, as they writhed and jerked their limbs like puppets in the hands of a crazy puppet-master, the Fritzes forgotten now.

De la Mazière did not give them a chance to recover or summon help from farther up the street, now practically blocked by the fiercely burning Stuka. Gasping for breath, hot sweat pouring down his face, he gasped, 'After me . . . quick . . . not a minute to lose . . . *After me!*'

The other two needed no urging. Their luck had held, true, but they knew it would—*could*—not last much longer. The three of them started running from the confusion behind them. Blinding flashes, explosions, rifle shots, groans, curses, stumbling writhing figures, dying on their feet, outlined stark black by the crackling vicious orange flame.

'*Stoi!*' A nervous voice commanded to their right.

An old woman was standing there, holding a rifle much too large for her skinny frame.

Hannemann didn't hesitate. He kicked the old woman in the right shin. She howled with pain, her stainless steel false teeth bulging stupidly from between her lips. She let go of the old rifle and Hannemann caught it neatly. Then they were off, knowing that they were lost in the middle of this vast country, every man's hand against them. A moment later the forest had swallowed them up.

CHAPTER 2

MARTIN BORMANN, the Führer's secretary, looking like an under-sized run-down boxer, had been laying down the law, in between greedy bites at a stick of salami, as they had waited for the audience. 'I'm a Mecklenburger myself, you know, gentlemen. I know all about those sub-humans in the East.' He had indicated the general direction of Russia. 'For nearly a thousand years, the Slavs lived in my native province till we Germans kicked them out, lock, stock and barrel, back to their own bogs and swamps.' He had taken another tremendous bite at the sausage, watched in horrified fascination by the elegantly uniformed officers with the crimson stripe of the staff down the side of their trousers. 'Since that time, good honest German peasants have farmed Mecklenburg, generation after generation of them. Now, *meine Herren*, if we don't stop the Red devils this summer, it won't be just their own damned country they'll conquer back, but Poland and after that East Prussia, the holy soil of the Reich itself! They won't stop there either. Then will come Brandenburg . . . Mecklenburg. My native province will be Slav again after one thousand years, imagine that.' He had ended his impromptu lecture with a belch and had hastily swallowed the last of his forbidden sausage (for the Führer thought his secretary was as vegetarian as himself) in the same instant that the great doors had been swung open and the giant black-clad SS adjutant had announced. '*Herr Oberst Greim! Der Führer lässt bitten!*'

Greim clicked to attention. Two SS officers at his side did likewise. A whispered command and, with his hat clasped beneath his right arm, the three of them stepped off as one, marching into the presence of the 'Greatest Captain of All Times'.

Hastily Adolf Hitler took off his nickel-rimmed spectacles in which it was forbidden to photograph him and, dismissing the brass around him with a wave of his pudgy yellow hand, advanced on Greim. 'My dear, dear Colonel,' he said in his thick throaty Upper Austrian voice. 'How good of you to come!'

Greim wasn't flattered. It had been 'good' of him to come. When Adolf Hitler summoned, that was that. There were no two ways about it. Numbly he allowed his hand to be taken by the Führer and waited for the reason for this strange summons, all the way from Russia to East Prussia. It came with startling suddenness. 'Greim,' Hitler barked, 'what's wrong with my Stuka?'

Greim had heard about Hitler's surprise questions. He wasn't taken off guard, knowing that the high-ranking staff officers deeper in the big room were watching expectantly, waiting for him to be cut down to size. Promptly, he answered. '*Mein Führer*, the Stuka is simply too old.'

Hitler did not seem surprised. 'Yes?' he said encouragingly.

'Too slow.'

'And?'

'Too under-armoured and virtually ineffective against the main target—enemy tanks.'

Behind Hitler, his officers looked serious, as if he were going too far now. But Hitler did not seem to mind. Instead he said easily. 'Could you explain in more detail, my dear, Greim?'

'*Jawohl, mein Führer*.'

It was an opportunity Greim had been waiting for since 1942 when the slaughter of the Stukas had commenced and Goering had not had the strength of character to admit that the dive bomber was obsolescent and needed replacing. Instead, he had sent eager young men to their deaths as pilots in a machine that had already had its day back in late 1940.

'Sir, a Soviet armoured attack these days is a clever mix of tanks and anti-aircraft guns. If we do not find the enemy tanks at once—and the Russians are past masters at camouflage—the flak slaughters us. We are slow and our pilots have not got armoured seats.' He had paused and let his words sink in.

Behind, one or two of the staff officers tut-tutted under their breath; one simply did not talk to the Führer like this. Bad news always had to be kept from him.

Greim had ignored their disapproval and continued. 'Of course, we have learned from our mistakes. Skill, *mein Führer*, is often the result of getting hurt. We have discovered that it is wiser to fly below the line of the flak's trajectory. We have learned that the Russian T-34s are equipped with smoke shells to imitate a conflagration so that we will think they have already been hit and are on fire. We have learned that the Russian tanks are most vulnerable from the stern. It is *there* that the engine is housed and in order to cool this engine, the armour plating is at its thinnest. It is also perforated with large holes to further assist this cooling process. In addition, where there is an engine there is also gas. Hit the engine and, if you're lucky, the gas will explode and set the monster ablaze.' He had paused and let them wait for his punch-line.

'Excellent, excellent, Greim,' Hitler had said, his pudgy sallow face glowing, 'this is the real essence of aerial combat. But please continue.'

'But that is the real problem, *mein Führer*,' Greim had snapped, '*hitting* the enemy tank!'

'What do you mean?'

'Well, sir, it is no use your bomb exploding around the tank. Its sides are too heavily armoured. All a bomb does, falling, say, fifty metres away, is to shake up the crew. Give them a bad headache at the most.'

His craggy, scarred face had cracked into a grin and the staff officers had frowned. But Hitler had shared his smile and had laid his hand on Greim's affectionately. Later Greim would realise that Hitler had been leading him on all the while; he had been waiting for exactly this moment when

Greim had come to the main defect of the vaunted dive-bomber.

'So in essence, my flying artillery, Colonel Greim,' he had prompted, his eyes beginning to flash with that old fire of his with which he had roused the mob back in the old days at the annual Nuremburg Party Rallies, 'can no longer hit its target effectively.'

'Exactly, sir. If we fly too high, the flak gets us. If we fly below the flak, we probably miss our target. If we fly at ground level, to make quite sure of hitting the enemy tank, mostly likely, *we get blown up by the explosion of our bomb!*'

'Exceedingly well put, Greim!' Hitler had said enthusiastically. 'It is exactly what my own investigations have revealed. Yet, let me put this question to you, my dear Greim.' He had fixed Greim with that look of his, which so many German officers thought—even swore—had an hypnotic effect, though Greim felt no magic stir within him at that brooding, penetrating gaze. 'Is the concept of flying artillery, especially in attacking enemy armoured formations, still viable?'

'Yes, my Führer,' he had answered promptly. 'In the attack, flying artillery is essential, if we are to ensure that the attacking infantry is to advance against enemy armour, as soon as their own land-based field artillery has to cease firing in case its shells hit its own men. But the Stuka and the bomb are not the right weapon,' he had ended doggedly.

'*Aber Mein Führer*—' the bemedalled, elegantly uniformed representative of the Luftwaffe had gasped; and *Reichsführer* Heinrich Himmler had flashed Greim a lethal look, his sallow schoolmaster's face suddenly flushed. 'The officers of the First SS Stuka Group are valiant men, worthy representatives of my Armed SS. They do not fear to die for the cause of our beloved Germany, *mein Führer*!'

Hitler had held up his hand for silence, in no way moved by Greim's bluntness or the outrage of his officers, particularly the head of the Armed SS, Himmler. It had been then that

Greim knew this whole business had been stage-managed and that the cunning old fox Hitler had had something up his damned greasy sleeve all the time.

'If . . . if, *Oberst* Greim,' Hitler had begun slowly, savouring what was to come, 'a new Stuka, its speed improved considerably, the pilot and gunner positions heavily armoured so that both crew members would be protected from the flak, if I could give you these things—'

'But the bomb, *mein Führer!*' Greim had objected impatiently.

Hitler had smiled, and said simply, 'But there will be no bomb!'

'*No bomb!*'

'Yes, my dear Greim. All winter we have been experimenting with a totally new type of Stuka. I think the experimenters at Rechlin have a pet name for it. 'He had paused. 'Cannonbird, they call it, It believe. Yes, that's it—*the cannonbird!* Now this is what we have done. . . .'

Even as Adolf Hitler had begun to explain in that sudden, almost boyish enthusiasm of his, Greim's heart had sunk. Whatever the 'cannonbird' was, it meant one thing and one thing only for 1st SS Stuka Group. *They were going back to Russia.* . . .

'*Achtung!*' The harsh metallic voice echoed and re-echoed across Rechlin Experimental Field.

Lying or kneeling on the parched grass, the waiting men narrowed their eyes against the glare. It cut the eye like the blade of a sharp knife. Blue heat ripples rose in a steady stream over the target. Far to the west, there was the muted sound of aircraft engines.

Colonel Greim, standing next to Karst and von Einem, raised his glasses, and stared at the glaring blue horizon. Two tiny black dots had appeared out of nowhere. '*Das sind sie!*' Karst snapped excitedly, taking his gaze off the captured T-

34s which were moored in the target area right in the centre of the field. '*Die Kannonenvoegel!*'

Greim grunted and watched the two sinister black dots grow ever larger in the gleaming circles of calibrated glass. This was it.

'For the last three months, we have been trying various combinations and calibres, gentlemen,' the unseen officer commented over the PA system. 'We have had many setbacks. Sometimes the calibre was too weak and ineffective. Sometimes too high and dangerous for the plane. But now we think that we have got the mix just right.'

Sprawled next to 'Papa' Diercks, Slack Arse Schmidt growled, 'The only mix, comrade, I could use at this shitting moment, is a big fat blonde—with no drawers on—and a barrel of ice-cold suds! God, it's hot!'

Papa grinned evilly and said, 'I know what you mean, Slack Arse. I've got so much ink in my fountain pen, I just don't know who to write to first.' He grabbed the front of his grey trousers melodramatically and gave a fake moan.

'Get off,' Slack Arse snorted. 'You had it up last when the Kaiser was still fucking up things in the Reich.' He scratched his cropped head in bewilderment and for good measure, bored his little finger into his right ear to excavate some hard wax that lay there and had been bothering him all morning. 'All the same, Papa, I'd like to know why we're confined to Rechlin Field like this, with all that free German gash just waiting for us outside, all nice, juicy and willing. We ain't seen no secrets, have we?'

Before Diercks could answer, the harsh metallic voice of the unseen commentator boomed, 'Now they are coming in for the attack, gentlemen, at approximately fifty metres above ground level.'

There were gasps of surprise, even shock, on all sides. '*Fifty shitting metres!*' someone cried in utter disbelief. 'Those Stuka jockeys must be crazy up there! They're gonna shoot themselves down if they drop dombs at the target from that height! Absolutely *meschugge*!'

Greim gasped, as he saw the two long sinister objects hanging beneath the gull-like wings of the first Stuka. Now he understood what the announcer had meant by 'calibre'. The Stuka, a bright gleaming silver, straight from the factory by the look of it, was not going to *bomb* the T-34s. It was going to *shoot* at them. Those long objects were anti-tank cannon!

On cue, the announcer said triumphantly, 'Both planes are armed with the latest 37mm cannon. We have experimented with the 20mm version, but it was too light. The 75mm version can knock out any known tank, but it makes the plane too slow and ponderous. We think the 37mm is the one.'

Next instant even the PA system was drowned by the roar of the silver Stuka racing into the attack. It skimmed across the parched field, its prop sweeping the grass in crazy waves, at 400 kilometres an hour. The whole world seemed filled with the mad racket of its engine. Greim tensed. It was now or never. If the pilot didn't fire soon, he'd smack right into the first of the T-34s.

A sudden spurt of flame. The pilot throttled back as the first brown streak shot from beneath his port wing. Abruptly the shell slammed into the T-34. It rocked, rearing up on its rear sprocket like a wild horse being put to the saddle for the first time. Suddenly its turret was flying lazily through the air, all ten tons of it, whirling round and round, as the next Stuka came belting in.

Its twin 37mms belched steel. The second T-34 took both shells to the left rear. There was a terrible, hollow boom of steel striking steel. Next moment the whole tank disintegrated. One moment the T-34 was there; the next it wasn't. When the smoke had cleared, all that remained was a heap of jumbled smoking wreckage with one lone bogie wheel trundling off aimlessly into the distance.

For what seemed an eternity, there was a heavy silence among the awed spectators, as they stared unbelievingly at the smoking ruins. The Stukas roared high into the burning blue sky, rolling ecstastically in a flash of bright silver at their success. Suddenly the spell was broken. A wild cheer broke out. Men slapped each other on the back, as if they personally had been responsible for the success of the Stuka attack. Others threw their caps into the air, yelling like drunken idiots.

Acting Captain Baron Karst swung round to face the keen-faced young fanatics of the SS, ignoring Colonel Greim. 'So comrades, what do you say now?' he cried boldly, his icy-blue eyes flashing fire. 'Is the day of the Stuka over, eh?'

'*No! no!*' they yelled back hoarsely, their eyes as fanatical as his, as to the rear at the control tower, the PA system started to blast out the *March of the Stukas*, all blaring brass and Wagnerian fury.

Spontaneously, clicking to attention, heads thrown back, eyes blazing with almost crazed pride, a score of hoarse young voices broke into that song of battle—and death.

> '*STUKA . . . STUKA . . . STUKA!*
> *Hawks of death . . . Steel, blood, and fury . . .*
> *Germany's sword . . . Germany's destiny . . .*
> *Striking east . . . striking west . . .*
> *Ever victorious, ever glorious . . .*
> *Death is our companion . . . blood our colour . . . steel our*
>   *weapon . . .*
> *STUKA . . . STUKA . . . STUKA!*'

Colonel Greim hardly heard that bold, vainglorious, fatalistic chant, punctuated by the stamp of the young men's booted right feet, as he walked slowly back to the control tower. His mind was too full of other things. So they were Hitler's 'cannonbirds'. Now he understood. Hitler had given his 'flying artillery' a new weapon, a cannon instead of a bomb. Hitler was going over to the offensive again and he wanted the Stuka to lead his armoured blitzkrieg as in the glorious days of 1940. That was why the boffins at Rechlin Field had been experimenting all winter with this 'cannonbird'. That was what all this was about—the summons to the FHQ, the sudden transfer of the 1st SS Stuka Group from Russia, the secrecy and the influx of eager young pilots straight from the Reich's training schools.

Greim halted and, biting his lip in doubt, stared at these bold young men, flushed with pride and National Socialist arrogance.

Did they know at this minute, as they bellowed out those brave words, how many other bold young men in their dashing black leather tunics had preceded them with that same defiant song on their lips? Did they know how tragically so many of those same men had vanished into the wastes of Russia for a cause that was no longer noble, but simply aggressive, greedy and cruel?

Of course not. Young men in a hurry for desperate glory never did think. It had always been thus. Instead they simply acted—and died.

Sadly Greim shook his head and went on his way, followed by the mocking words of that bold song of death. *'Death is our companion . . . blood our colour . . . steel our weapon . . . STUKA! STUKA! STUKA!'*

CHAPTER 3

'*IVANS!*' Hannemann hissed.

In spite of their weariness, the three of them dropped to the ground immediately, with Hanno von Heiter pressing his hand automatically over Fifi's muzzle to prevent her from yapping.

Cautiously, de la Mazière wriggled his way forward through the skeletal undergrowth to where Hannemann sprawled, his uniform ragged, scorched and torn, rifle grasped in hands like small steam shovels. He nodded his head up the track. 'There.'

De la Mazière stared ahead while Hanno clutched his absurd dog and waited fearfully for their verdict.

They had been running for three days now. Blundering blindly through field and forest, snatching water from puddles, grabbing what they could find from the frozen earth, their iron ration of chocolate greedily devoured long ago, they had realised the German Army had not held the Russians on the Dnieper after all. The retreat was on again and they were in some kind of limbo, a no-man's land between the retreating Wehrmacht and the first Red Army patrols, assisted by the partisans who seemed to be everywhere, constantly blocking the fugitives' attempts to link up with their own forces.

Everywhere on their blind progress westwards, they had come across evidence of those final, brief, vicious skirmishes between their own soldiers and the enemy. A hastily improvised road block and the familiar signs of another battle lost by the Wehrmacht. Scattered helmets, a sprinkle of ammunition, a smashed machine-gun, a smouldering truck or tank, the ripped-off uniform sleeve or trouser leg, where someone's wounds had been hastily dressed—and the dead, abandoned in the ditches like bundles of wet rags. They were like picnic grounds where the careless picnickers would never yawn awake again.

Now after a cold exhausted morning of thrashing their way through a swampy morass with their rumbling stomachs doing what Hannemann called, 'shitting flip-flops from shitting hunger—*Christ, have I got cabbage-steam!*'* they had emerged joyfully onto the track—to find it blocked yet once again by the enemy.

'Look a mixed bunch to me, sir,' Hannemann whispered, eyes narrowed as he took in the men standing 200 metres away smoking fitfully and saying little, like men who had already done a hard day's work and were conserving their energy.

De la Mazière nodded his agreement, as he surveyed the group. Most of them were in the shabby clothes, peaked caps and rucksacks of the partisans, heavy old-fashioned rifles over their shoulders; but two or three of them were in the earth-brown tunics of the Red Army and the tallest wore one of the leather-padded helmets of the Russian Tank Corps.

For a moment or two, his thought processes slowed down by hunger, de la Mazière wondered why. Then he saw the low shape of a T-34 to the left of the track, its deck and long overhanging 75mm cannon hung with branches and camouflage nets. As always the Russians, even in victory, took care to conceal their tanks, as if a squadron of Stukas might fall out of the sky at any moment. De la Mazière's, begrimed forehead wrinkled in a frown, as he stared at the tank and the group of Russians opposite it.

'Hannemann,' he said softly.

'Sir?'

'What do you think of our chances of riding jockey?'

'Riding jockey, sir?'

'*Jawohl*. On that tank,' de la Mazière answered the

---

*German soldiers' slang for hunger

puzzled question, a new determination in his voice. 'We've had it without wheels.'

'You can say that again, sir,' Hannemann agreed with a heartfelt sigh. 'My poor aching dogs never stop barking! But how are we gonna nobble that tank, sir? There are twenty or more of the Popov pigs and only three of us—and a dog, of course,' he added with a weak attempt at humour.

'Through the dog.'

Hannemann looked at the tall gaunt officer, as if he had suddenly gone mad. 'Did I hear you right, sir? Through that pansified pissy frog poddle?'

'You did. If that—*thing*—can distract them for a few minutes, we can do it. I hope. Come on, let's get back to Captain von Heiter and I'll explain how.'

'But Detlev,' Hanno protested, clutching the poodle to his chest protectively, 'what if things go wrong? What about Fifi then?' De la Mazière sighed wearily. In his present state it had taken a real effort of will to explain his plan to Hanno; now he was kicking up such a fuss all for the sake of the stupid little dog.

Up the trail a group of the Russians had started a fire and were frying meat over its flame on their entrenching tools. The tantalising smell was wafting their way, making his stomach rumble furiously with desire.

'God in heaven,' Hannemann growled at his side, 'must they? My chin water's running down like the shitting old Rhine river! Hell, am I hungry!'

'Now listen, Hanno,' de la Mazière said with determination. 'Fifi's got to take her chance, just like the rest of us. If we don't make it now, we'll all go hop, including that precious shitting pooch of yours!'

'But she's so delicate, Detlev,' Hanno said, stroking his mascot lovingly, naked fear in his eyes at the thought of losing his dog. 'Without her, God knows what I'd do?'

'You'd be like we are all going to be,' de la Mazière snapped, losing his patience, '*looking at the potatoes from beneath two metres of Russian earth*! For God's sake, don't go on about the little beast. Let's get on with it.'

'Oh, all right,' Hanno gave in. 'But you will take care, won't you?'

'Of course, we will, sir,' Hannemann answered, licking cracked lips at the thought of that meat. At this moment he would have given a whole drawerful of medals for one big bite of hot meat. 'Don't you worry.'

'Good,' de la Mazière announced, slipping the safety catch off his Schmeisser, while Hannemann unslung his captured Russian rifle. They weren't much against twenty-odd armed Ivans but if they did achieve surprise, they might just pull it off. 'Give us five minutes to get into position. As soon as you hear the hoot of the owl, which will be me, let the dog off the leash.'

'And tell her, sir,' Hannemann added cheerfully, 'there'll be a nice juicy bone in it for her, if she does her stuff correct like.' Hanno patted the silly dog, its normally elegantly clipped and well-washed coat, now dirty, its legs begrimed with hardened black mud. 'All right. But I do hope that everything will go off all right.'

De la Mazière rose to his feet and growled angrily. 'Well, you could at least wish us good luck, Hanno.'

With that, he was crawling on all fours through the undergrowth, placing his hands and knees down as carefully as if he were moving across a sea of eggshells. Behind him, Hannemann did the same, face set and determined. A moment later the two of them had disappeared, leaving Hanno and the dog alone.

'Great crap on the Christmas tree!' de la Mazière cursed and stared up at the sheer shale face that had appeared, as if out of nowhere, concealed as it had been at their starting point by the firs.

'Now what, sir?' Hannemann hissed, for the Russians were

on the other side of the obstacle and he could hear the tempting sizzle of the frying meat and their soft chatter. He could smell them, too, that typical odour of Russian, a compound of sweat, animal droppings and black *marhorka* tobacco.

Miserably, de la Mazière stared up at the cliff, the energy and hope draining out of his emaciated weary body, as if a tap had been opened. He sighed. 'There's only one way. We've got to climb it.'

'Great flying pisspots, sir!' Hannemann objected. 'It's a good thirty metres high—and I get dizzy at heights. Specially when I have my monthlies,' he added with a weak attempt at his old humour, 'such as now.'

De la Mazière ignored the comment. 'Come on,' he said glumly, slinging his machine-pistol. 'Give me a heave up. Let's have a go at the shitting thing. There's no other way.'

Willingly Hannemann bent, hands on his knees, and offered his broad back to the officer. De la Mazière stepped on it, hearing Hannemann grunt under the strain. He reached up his hand, yelping a little as the sharp blue shale sliced at his searching fingers, telling himself that it was almost suicidal to be attempting the climb within earshot of the Ivans.

Suddenly his probing hand found a hold. A jug handle. Hastily he curled the fingers of one hand about it and letting go, heaved his feet up until he found a niche to rest them on. 'Hannemann,' he whispered urgently, 'toss up your rifle.'

'Sir.'

With his one free hand, hardly daring to breathe, de la Mazière felt behind his back until his fingers curled around Hannemann's weapon. Squirming and wriggling, he managed to get it around his neck before proceeding on the next stage of his climb.

On the other side of the cliff face, he could hear someone singing softly accompanied by the sound of tapping metal, a bayonet perhaps. De la Mazière prayed that the singer would not stop. The sad song might just drown the terrible racket he seemed to be making, as he laboured upwards.

Now he was sweating profusely, trying to ignore the blazing agony of his shoulder muscles. His breath came in gasps. More than once he shook his tormented face to dislodge the beads of sweat constantly threatening to blind him. He paused for breath on a tiny ledge. Then, with the utmost caution, turned and released one end of the rifle sling. Letting it dangle as far as he could reach, and praying that his foothold would not give way, he whispered, 'All right, Hannemann, grab hold. Up you come.' he took the strain.

Hannemann cursed as he dislodged a shower of pebbles, but for such a big man, he managed surprisingly well, clambering up the sheer face like a trained climber, knowing that de la Mazière could not hold him for long. He swung himself on to the ledge next to the officer, just as the latter had told himself that he couldn't hold Hannemann a moment longer. For what seemed an age, the two ragged fugitives knelt there as if in prayer, their shoulders heaving.

Finally, with an effort, de la Mazière pulled himself together. There were still about ten metres to go. 'All right, Hannemann, on your knees. This is the last bit of the swine.'

Obediently Hannemann bent and gingerly, for the ledge was very narrow, de la Mazière mounted his back and reached upwards as far as he could. He found a vertical crack, and crammed his fingertips into it urgently. For a moment he hung there, the strain on his fingertips almost unbearable. A finger nail cracked. An excruciating pain shot through his arm in fiery waves. He almost blacked out. The blood streamed down his hand. His blood-wet fingers beginning to slip, de la Mazière lurched forward—and found a foot-hole.

He started to move. Once his upper body seemed to be suspended in space, his only hold a nick in the rock for his right foot. Just as he felt he must slip down the rock face to the ground below, he found another hold and was moving upwards again, body racked with pain, his breath coming from lungs that wheezed like cracked leathern bellows. And then he had done it. He dragged Hannemann after him, and the two of them sprawled high above the Russians, their hearts beating like piledrivers, their bodies trembling. They were at the top!

There it was. There was no mistaking it: the agreed signal. The hoot of an owl. Hanno von Heiter swallowed hard. Fondly he kissed the little dog, feeling its skinny body trembling in his grasp. '*Cherche,*' he commanded, putting it on the ground, '*cherche Oncle Detlev.*'

The dog growled and refused to budge from his side, although his master was using French, which he did only when he had something important to communicate to Fifi; after all, she had been born in France. Fifi cowered, floppy ears pinned close to her skull and whimpered softly.

'*Allez vite, Fifi!*' Hanno urged miserably, knowing that his mascot was just as scared as he was. '*Allez!*'

The 'owl' hooted again.

Desperately Hanno struck the dog. 'Fuck off!' he commanded. 'Go on . . . earn your shitting keep, will you, Fifi! Go!'

Fifi gave him one last miserable look, then she was off reluctantly, trailing her stomach along the earth, as she crawled towards the Russians, earning her 'shitting keep' at last. Hanno bit his lip with worry. If she didn't make it, he knew he was finished.

'*Boshe moi!*' The first Russian, holding the glowing shovel cried in amazement at the sight, nearly losing his precious meat in the flames of the fire with surprise. 'Look, comrades! What in the name of the Holy Virgin of Kazan is *it*?'

All around him the partisans and the men of the Tank

Corps swung about, stopping their cooking, to stare at the strange creature advancing upon them with obvious reluctance along the trail.

'Is it some kind of small bear?' someone asked, as Fifi came ever closer, and made as if to unsling his rifle from his back.

'Idiot!' another answered. 'It's no bear. It's some kind of dog.'

'Dog!' A dozen bass voices exclaimed in disbelief and awe. '*That*—a dog!'

'*Da . . . da . . . Ya snayu*,' the one who had identified Fifi answered confidently. 'Look at the snout, and the tail.'

'But what happened to its head and legs?' someone objected. 'They've been curled . . . to look like some Moscow whore! Surely that can't be a dog?'

In the fashion of simple countrymen, which they all were, they crowded around the strange apparition, which now lay supine and trembling in the sticky mud, whimpering softly, as they prodded it and examined it, mouths gaping, as if it might well have just been dropped from the moon.

Twenty metres above them on the rock outcrop, de la Mazière nudged a tense Hannemann.

Hannemann nodded his understanding and raising his rifle, brought the circular sight round until the helmeted head of the Tank Corps was set firmly in the centre.

'A perfect target,' de la Mazière whispered as his finger whitened on the trigger of his Schmeisser. 'A wonderful group. If we pull this off, Hannemann, I'll never say another unkind word against that silly dog.'

Hannemann did not answer. He couldn't. He knew that if they didn't slaughter or knock out the Russians grouped around Fifi in their first burst, they'd be finished. Once the survivors scattered into the surrounding trees and began returning their fire, they'd never get out of the trap they had set for themselves. It would be curtains.

De la Mazière took first pressure, gaze fixed hypnotically on the crowd of Russians below. He said a quick prayer and, trying to control his breathing and the mad fluttering of his heart, he eased into second pressure.

The machine pistol burst into frenetic activity at his side. In a flash the peaceful scene below was transformed. The Russians didn't have a chance to react. They went down screaming, clutching the air, as if they were climbing the rungs of an invisible ladder, spinning in a wild whirl under the impact of the cruel steel at such close range, falling face-first into their own fires, while Fifi lay trembling at their dying feet, howling miserably, as if her heart were broken at being the cause of this merciless slaughter.

Carried away by the blood lust of battle, adrenaline spurting into his blood stream and filling him with new energy, de la Mazière dropped from rock to rock, firing quick controlled short bursts from the hip as he did so, while above Hannemann, on his feet now, gave him covering fire, snapping off shots to left and right whenever a Russian attempted to break away from that circle of death. Hanno von Heiter came running up the trail, pistol in hand.

A partisan attempted to bolt towards him. Perhaps he thought Hanno was a fellow partisan coming to help him. Von Heiter paused, one arm thrust behind him, as if on the range back in the Fatherland, and pressed his trigger. The slug smacked right into the running man's face. He gave a terrible howl as he swayed for what seemed an age, his features dripping on to his chest like melting red wax.

Hannemann came tumbling down the rocks, as de la Mazière finished off the survivors mercilessly from ten metres' range, his face crimson and contorted with an almost unbearable excitement, eyes glittering like those of a madman.

A couple of the Russians, surrounded by their dead and dying comrades piled up like human logs, threw down their weapons and even as they died, threw up their hands in the classic posture of supplication. It was only when all the Russians were down, already dead or writhing in their death throes, and their weapons clicked purposelessly, signifying that all their ammunition was gone, that they lowered their weapons, blinking, as they tried to comprehend just what happened on that gloomy trail. Like sleepwalkers, they staggered forward, uttering meaningless noises, shaking their heads constantly, as if fighting to throw off sleep and wake from their strange trancelike state.

In the end it was Fifi's wild barking, an urgent appeal for attention, which snapped them out of it. Suddenly their mood was one of awe at the slaughter they had brought about, and elation that they had done it. They had knocked out the Ivans—and they had wheels!

In the manner of young men, long brutalised by combat, knowing that their own lives would be of short duration, too—for they, too, would end like this, violently done to death in some nameless arsehole of the world—they grabbed the half-cooked pieces of meat out of the dead men's lifeless hands and wolfed them down, the grease running down their bearded chins, laughing and chortling as they savoured the precious food, bending here and there to loot the Russians' rucksacks for cigarettes and vodka, turning the bodies hither and thither carelessly with the toes of their boots, no longer regarding the dead Russians as human beings like themselves but as 'things'. And at their feet, Fifi whimpered unheeded.

Ten minutes later they were gone in a cloud of blue smoke and an awkward flurry of mud and pebbles, as Hannemann at the controls swung the T-34 on to the main trail. Behind them they left the Russians to stiffen in the cold breeze. . . .

CHAPTER 4

ALL THAT long hot April of 1943 they trained. Never before had the pilots and ground crews of the 1st SS Stuka Squadron trained so long and hard. From first light to dusk, Colonel Greim kept his men on the move, knowing that he did not have much time. The call to action would come all too soon.

The volunteers from the SS flying school were eager to take over the controls of the new Stukas. Their instructors had told them that the cannonbird was a war-winning weapon. It would achieve final victory for Germany in the East. At last they would be able to stop the flood of enemy armour which was threatening to swamp Central Europe and run right on to the 'holy soil' of the Reich itself. For them the cannonbird meant fame and promotion: a chance to restore their bankrupt family fortunes. They burned with desire to go into action with the new wonder weapon.

But Colonel Greim, although he heartily disliked the breed, did not allow their enthusiasm to blind them to the realities of the war on the Eastern Front. In spite of its new 'wonder weapon', it was still the same old Stuka, easy meat for Russian fighters, when handled by an inexperienced young pilot such as these.

Eight hours a day, far exceeding the flying norm in the other squadrons, his young bloods were kept at it: formation flying, diving, bombing, gunnery. The 1st SS Stuka Group flew as if they were already at the front on ops, with two Messerschmitts, 'borrowed'—for a truckload of looted Russian vodka—from a nearby fighter-squadron, acting as Russian interceptors and firing live ammunition at the massed Stuka formations.

In the evening, the newcomers staggered from their planes on legs that seemed to be made of india-rubber, numb with fatigue, reviving themselves by plunging their crimson faces into pails of ice-cold water, only to find themselves suddenly transformed into infantry, running over the sun-baked fields with twenty kilos of heavy equipment strapped to their weary, pain-racked bodies, urged on mercilessly by Baron Karst and the handful of veterans. '*Come on, you piss pansies, at the double Los . . . los . . . . Call yourself the élite . . . I've shat better turds . .* !' and the rest of the usual cruel litany of contempt.

Colonel Greim did not approve, but he knew it was necessary. His young pilots not only had to be expert fliers, but also at the height of their physical fitness for whatever ordeal lay before them. In Russia, for he had guessed it was in that accursed country the new wonder weapon would be employed, they would need all the strength and stamina they could muster.

Neither did his ground crews escape, veterans of Spain and four years of war as most of them were. Stripped to the waist, bodies lean and bronzed, they lugged bombs and shells by the hour, sweating and cursing as Papa Diercks tongue-lashed them, urging them to ever greater speed as one squadron had its supply of shells for the cannon renewed while another hovered above in the perfect blue sky, ready to land. '*Tempo! Tempo!*' he would cry at the sweat-glazed, red-faced mechanics and armourers in their shorts and tennis shoes, timing them with his stop-watch, 'Get those shells in there! Hurry it up now! Too much of the old one-handed widow at night, I'll be bound! *MOVE IT!*'

Each Saturday Greim instituted a live-firing display so that the young pilots could show off their progress and the ground crews could see what all their back-breaking effort was about.

For a few moments the massed Stuka squadrons, nearly one hundred planes in all, would hover, sinister, threatening, black against the burning blue wash of the afternoon sky, before falling out of the heavens at an impossible speed. Sirens howling, engines racing, they would fall, one after the other, as if they would never stop and plummet into the earth, levelling out at tree-top height, to come flashing by, their great cannon thumping. While the watching ground crew gasped, the white blur of tracer shells would hiss towards the tanks being used as targets. A boom of metal on metal. A blast of hot air which would have the spectators gasping and choking for breath. And the cannonbird would be soaring joyously into the burning blue sky, a great silver steaming hole skewered through the metal side of the tank.

By the time a whole squadron had worked the target over, it would be a mess of broken, confused smoking metal, no longer recognisable as a fighting vehicle, and the ground crews, even the most jaded and war-weary of them, would be on their feet, whistling and applauding the roaring, diving, all-powerful cannonbirds.

Captain Baron Karst's lectures on 'National Socialist Philosophy', which *Reichsführer SS* Heinrich Himmler had now insisted would be introduced to all SS units, even those at the front, met with much less enthusiasm. 'The men are slack, sir!' he had barked to Colonel Greim when the subject had been raised at their regular morning meeting. 'They have little concept of what this war is about. Some of them think it is only an excuse for getting away from their wives so that they can whore around and get drunk each night.'

Colonel Greim had smiled knowingly and asked in his deceptively mild manner, 'And what is it—the war, I mean—about, Karst?'

'Germany's future, sir,' he had snapped promptly. 'A *new* Europe with a *new* belief—a totally *New* Order to sweep the old decadence and corruption away for good. In essence, sir, our Führer Adolf Hitler'—and he had shot to attention at the very mention of that holy name—'is trying to create a new man, hard ruthless, selfless, determined to sacrifice all, his life if necessary, for the cause of Greater Germany!' Baron Karst's face had glowed with pride.

For his part, Colonel Greim had cast a cynical glance out of the window of his office at the tough faces of his 'old hares' who had been with him ever since Spain and told himself, 'That'll be the day.'

Thus had commenced the 'Karst Capers', as the crewmen called his talks, through which most of them slept if they could manage it, full of the differences between Jewish and Aryan tibia and the cephalic index of Indo-Germanic skulls.

As Slack Arse Schmidt complained to Papa Diercks over a half-litre of *Loewenbraeu* in the sergeants' mess after one such boring lecture on national socialist cultural nonsense, 'What in three devils' name has the length of a Yid's foreskin got to do with the shitting war, Papa? The chief rabbi can dock the end off'n my salami this very minute if it'd make me a non-Aryan and keep me from ever going back to shitting Popovland.' With an angry gesture he indicated the east and the brutal, bloody war being waged there. 'What a lot of crappy bloodshit!'

Papa Diercks smiled in that wise old, tolerant way of his and said, 'Don't knock it, Slack Arse. Let the black bastard talk about foreskins and perverted foreign fornication to his heart's content. The longer he talks, the longer we'll be here, old house. Here we are nice and comfy in the Homeland. No Popovs! No bees! No cabbage-steam! Here it's all sausage and sauerkraut, suds and sex.' He beamed winningly at his old comrade. 'I'm happy. You're happy. So what?'

Slack Arse Schmidt looked darkly above his mug at the other man's smiling old face, his mind still full of poor dead Hannemann and all the rest of his pals he had left in Russia. 'So what?' he grunted, 'I'll tell you so what, Papa!' He aimed a long, almost accusing forefinger at the other NCO and said challengingly, 'How long's it all gonna last? Ay, Papa, tell me that. *How long?*'

'*How long?*' It was a question that occupied others too. One afternoon, Colonel Greim and von Einem, still limping from his foot wound, stood in the shade of the officers' mess, watching as the massed formations of American fortresses headed for Berlin for yet another daylight raid. Like silver spiders they drew their vapour trails across the blue sky, peppered here and there by the drifting puff-balls of brown smoke. Fighters were rising to meet them from the field from which they 'borrowed' their Messerschmitts, white tracer already curving towards the bombers.

But the Americans did not deign even to reply with their massed machine-guns. They merely tightened their formation and the German fighters buzzed around helplessly like horseflies trying to goad a horse into bolting with their stings—and failing badly.

Then they were gone, the fighters trailing after them helplessly, plunging and curving impotently, as if willing one of the great silver birds to take up the challenge.

'How long, sir?' Von Einem whispered, almost as if he were speaking to himself.

'How long, *what?*' Greim dabbed his brow with his silk handkerchief and stared at von Einem. The pilot had aged ten years in the last months. Once he had been as brash, bold and cocky as the greenbeaks straight from the SS training schools, full of their typical aristocratic arrogance. Now he had become withdrawn, not even letting off steam in the mess when drunk, as others did when their nerve had started to go, hurling glasses at the mirrors, wrecking the furniture, setting light to the mess waiter's trousers and all the rest of those cruel, infantile tricks that desperate young men reaching the end of their tether indulge in.

Von Einem nodded his head in the direction of the disappearing Fortresses. 'How long can we stand up against the flying furniture vans* and the Tommies by night? The populace can only take so much from those Ami air gangsters. You can feel the mood of the Homeland has changed

*Air force slang for the Flying Fortress

drastically since Stalingrad, sir.' He frowned. In the sky one of the fighters from the nearby field was coming in awkwardly, wobbling from side to side, trailing brilliant white smoke behind it. It had been badly hit.

'Go on,' Greim urged, wondering yet again at the change in his SS pilots' mood and attitude. Even they were beginning to learn to face hard facts, well, at least, the veterans among them.

'And how long are we going to stay here for, sir?' In spite of the heat of the afternoon, von Einem shivered and said by way of an apology, 'Louse must have run across my liver, sir.'

'Probably,' Greim agreed. 'How long, von Einem? Not much longer, is my guess. My private canaries in the Berlin Air Ministry aren't singing very much these days and that makes me suspicious that the balloon is going to go up soon. Why, von Einem, you've got enough tin on your chest already, haven't you?' He indicated the young veteran's bemedalled chest. 'Or are you becoming a glory-hunter again?'

Von Einem forced a weary smile. 'No, sir. I've had a noseful—right up to here.' He drew his forefinger under his nose to indicate the degree of his disgust. 'It's just that I'm hoping it won't be Popovland again.' He shivered once more dramatically, his skinny frame twitching for an instant as if he were suffering from a violent fever. 'Anywhere but Russia! Africa, Italy, France.'

Greim made a joke of it. 'France, von Einem! You must be crazy? They wouldn't sent us *there*! France is for senior staff officers to eat in classy Parisian restaurants and have classy chats about the cosmos with French intellectuals—and if they're lucky and are still capable,' he winked knowingly at the other officer, 'have classy love affairs with high-born French ladies. France isn't for the like of the 1st SS.'

'But Russia is, sir?' von Einem persisted, his face still set and dour.

Suddenly Greim himself was infected by the young pilot's

despondent mood, His face grew sombre. He nodded and said, 'Yes, von Einem, Russia is.'

Von Einem swallowed hard and said in a voice that was cracked and without hope, 'I thought so, sir.' He touched his hand to his cap that was set at that old reckless angle that they had once affected, those who had died these many months ago. 'Better get back to my squadron.'

'Of course, von Einem.' Automatically Greim touched his own cap and watched von Einem cross into the bright sunshine, his shoulders slumped, as if in defeat. The young pilot already had the mark of death upon him; he would not survive Russia this time.

Forty-eight hours later, one of his 'Berlin canaries' sang over the scrambler phone from the Air Ministry, but the song he trilled was not particularly pleasant. 'Citadel, they call it, old house,' he had informed a suddenly apprehensive Greim, 'Operation Citadel, and it's going to be a really big one this time. Seventeen hundred aircraft are going to be made available by Fat Hermann.* Imagine it, Walter, *seventeen hundred*, with a thousand of them bombers and ground attack aircraft! Believe me, old friend, it's going to be May 1940 all over again.**

His informant had chuckled hugely and Greim, face grim and anxious, could imagine his fat jowls wobbling with pleasure.

'Believe me, *altes Haus*, they won't stop us this time!'

Colonel Greim took a deep breath, as if it needed an effort to ask the simple question, 'The Russians?'

'Yes, the Ivans, Walter. Now we must really stop the rot that set in after Stalingrad, otherwise the buggers will be parading up the *Unter den Linden* and spoiling my love life. And we can't have that, can we, Walter?' Again the other man laughed happily, as if it all were a damn great joke.

*Nickname for Marshal Goering, head of the Luftwaffe
**The date of the German invasion of France

'Of course not, Fritz,' Greim answered dutifully and then put that overwhelming question, 'When?'

'Don't know exactly, Walter. This summer for certain, though. My guess is July or thereabouts.'

'July!' Greim echoed.

'At all events, you'll be summoned to Berlin to meet Fat Hermann with all the rest of the group commanders concerned. You'll find out exactly then, Walter. Looking forward to it. There's a nice little place I know here, just off the *Tirpitzufer*. No questions asked about ration cards or anything stupid like that. Finest French wines, too, God knows where they get them from! And if you fancy a lady of night for afterwards, you old dog, that can be arranged, too. . . .' Suddenly the good humour went out of the canary's voice to be replaced by bewilderment. 'Walter,' he rapped, 'Walter, are you still on the line? *Walter?*'

But Colonel Walter Greim was no longer listening, as he stood there, phone clasped in a suddenly sweaty hand, staring into nothingness . . .

CHAPTER 5

WITH THE roar of an infuriated beast, the bombardment commenced again. Suddenly from the whole length of the valley from north to south, came countless flashes of violent light like the mouths of giant blast furnaces spewing fire. The guns thundered. The earth shuddered. All at once, sounded the deafening, awesome drum-roll of the barrage. Soon the waiting infantry, crouching in front of the guns, would rise to their feet again and in a wave, the colour of the earth itself, would flood forward to the German positions. They had been doing so for two days now and the shattered, cratered lunar landscape to their front was littered with a carpet of bodies in their earth-coloured uniforms.

Hannemann squatted in the stinking, lice-infected bunker with the two officers, both as ragged and as dirty as he, and gnawed at the edge of the iron-hard loaf of black bread he had taken from the pack of a dead Russian. 'Are we gonna have a go this time, sir?' He looked at de la Mazière, his face painfully thin, dark circles underneath his eyes.

De la Mazière took his time, but then now everything, even a few simple words, took the greatest of effort. He found he could only speak in short measured phrases; he had not the strength or mental concentration to do more. They had been on the run for too long. 'Well, Hannemann. . . . We've got this far . . . the front line. . . . We don't want to . . . fuck it up . . . now.'

Hannemann passed his share of the bread to Hanno von Heiter, who tore off a piece weakly and handed it to the dog. Fifi started to chew the dark dough without enthusiasm or energy. She, too, was about at the end of her tether. 'Can't stop here much longer, sir,' Hannemann warned, as the thunder of the guns increased, and shell after shell screamed with an exultant shriek about their heads. 'They'll rumble us sooner or later.'

'I know . . . I know, Hannemann. It's a question of . . . correct timing. . . . If we go in with their . . . infantry attack . . . we chance the Ivans . . . discovering us. . . . If we wait till they are . . . driven back . . . we face sudden death at the . . . hands of our own people. . . . You know . . . how trigger-happy those front-line . . . stubble-hoppers are. . . . Shoot first . . . ask questions later. . . .' He gasped for breath at the effort of so much talking, his face an alarming chalk-colour under the grime. 'Pick the right time . . . important,' he choked.

The green and red alarm flares were hissing into the leaden sky all along the German front, as the infantrymen prepared for the fresh attack to come and summoned whatever reserves were still left. The artillery roared with renewed fury, the noise reaching a baleful, man-made tornado. In a minute it would stop and they would attack.

Hannemann bit his lip, knowing now that he had to bear the burden of command. Both officers were about finished and even de la Mazière's willpower was breaking. If they didn't manage to cross soon, the two of them would slump into a disastrous apathy which could only result in carelessness, capture and ultimate death. 'Listen,' he said, forgetting military courtesy now and dropping the 'sir'. 'It's this attack or never. At ten o'clock, over there,' he indicated a patch of shell-torn earth littered with bodies to his left, 'they seem to have stopped attacking the last couple of times.' He shrugged carelessly. 'Perhaps they took too many casualties there—the Popovs, I mean. It doesn't matter. Once they go in and get involved with out lads, we're taking that way.'

Hanno raised his head, but said nothing. De la Mazière managed a hoarse, 'But—'

Hannemann did not give him a chance to protest, 'Look, I took these from the T-34.' He opened his pocket and showed them the two smoke grenades he had taken from the Russian

tank which they had abandoned a couple of days before when
their fuel had run out. 'They'll give us some kind of cover, if
necessary.'

'But our people in the line?' de la Mazière managed to
object.

'We'll take that hurdle when we get to it. Now, dump
everything you don't need. Come on, get rid of that popgun.'
He nodded at the Schmeisser which de la Mazière still
carried. 'We haven't got any ammo for it anyhow.'

He shot a look at the dog and Hanno von Heiter followed
his gaze with sudden alarm. He pressed the poodle to his chest
protectively and Hannemann let it go. If he wanted to carry
the damned thing, let him. Besides there was no more time for
quarrelling about Fifi. Instead he took the rifle from his own
back and dropped it in the corner of the hole. In the Russian
lines, the whistles shrilled and officers bellowed hoarse
commands. In a minute they would be going into the attack
again. They had to be ready.

Over in the enemy positions there was drunken singing and
cheers of '*krasnya armya . . . slava krasnya armya slava. . . .*'
Hannemann nodded his approval. The officers were handing
out the vodka, getting the men pepped up for the ordeal to
come. It was all to the good. With a bit of luck, they'd be too
high to spot the intruders in their midst. He gripped the first
smoke grenade more tightly in a hand that was suddenly wet
with sweat. In a minute the attack would start.

'Get ready,' he whispered, eyeing the front, shrouded now
in thick rolling clouds of smoke, knowing that over there, so
tantalisingly close, there were men of his own country, who
spoke his own language, shared ideas and ideals. Now they
cowered and waited in their crazily rocking holes, some
already filled with the cruelly torn-apart dead of their
comrades.

Suddenly, the barrage stopped. Soviet infantry were too
poorly disciplined to follow a creeping barrage as could
German stubble-hoppers. There was a startling silence,

heavy with the roll and thunder of the booming echoes, dying away in the surrounding hills. But not for long.

Fur-hatted Russian commanders were springing out of their holes, waving their curved sabres and shouting commands. Whistles shrilled urgently. A youngster, fur cap set at the back of his blond curls in the bold Russian fashion, waved the blood-red flag of the Soviet Union. A great cheer rose from the earth-coloured ranks crawling out of their holes, long bayonets gleaming a dull silver. A bugle sounded sweet and clear, and they streamed forward, hundreds, perhaps thousands of them, calling that war cry of theirs in a deep, frightening bass. '*Urrah! Urrah! URRAH!*'

Hannemann looked no longer. '*Los!*' he hissed urgently, as the first rank, bayonets at the high port, stamped by their hiding place, the very earth seeming to tremble beneath their marching feet. 'Let's go!'

De la Mazière flashed a look at Hanno; then he wasted no further time. He pulled himself out of the hole, abruptly feeling naked and vulnerable, gasping already with the effort of the sudden move. Behind him Hanno von Heiter hugged his pet to his skinny chest and followed.

In front of them, through the wavering fronds of brown smoke, they glimpsed the Russian infantry advancing, still crying their '*urrah!*', but muted now, as if heard from a distance, their stocky bodies bent as if they were struggling against a strong wind.

Hannemann flashed a look behind. The second wave was still a hundred metres away. 'Come on,' he urged, 'let's go, and for shit's sake, keep up!' As an afterthought, he added, '*Please*, gentlemen!'

Limping miserably, trying to dodge the shell-holes, filled with scummy water and dead bodies, the three of them edged their way after the first rank, which was tensing even more as that first dreaded hysterical hiss of a German spandau cut the air and tracer started to wing its way in multi-coloured, smoking viciousness towards them.

Hannemann cursed to himself and thought it would be shitting supreme irony if he and the other two were slaughtered by their own people. But it was a chance they had to take.

The air was full of the hiss of tracer, the howls of spent slugs ricocheting off the rocks, the sudden screams and awful cries of those struck by the burning bullets. Officers bellowed orders. NCOs cursed and kicked the laggards, the ones already wanting to go to earth. The line, already showing ragged gaps, stumbled into an awkward, shambling run. The German fire intensified, seeming to merge into a frightening glowing wall. Still the Russian infantry kept on coming. Drunk or brave, or both, they ran into that burning sudden death, as the spandaus chattered on relentlessly, dying with the name of that monster Stalin on their lips, as if it were that of God Himself.

Hannemann pushed on, ignoring the '*wheep-wheep*' of the bullets. Once a burst ripped up the mud right in front of their feet. Hanno flopped, Fifi yelping in his arms. For a moment he sprawled in the black goo, head buried, as the bullets howled in their grating, shrieking descent all about them, de la Mazière swaying drunkenly.

Hannemann grabbed him by the scruff of the neck and raised him as if he were a child, the dog still yapping. 'Great God and All His Triangles!' he roared, face crimson with fury. 'Will you keep going! *Move it!*' He gave the young officer a shove and sent him staggering onwards. Mechanically de la Mazière followed, getting ever closer to that crazy maelstrom of flying steel. The Russian line was by now very thin, scattered groups of lonely men, soft human flesh quivering as the angry bullets cut the air all about them, alone among the noise and smoke lurching on in bewilderment, spurred forward by mad freaks of fancy until they, too, went down, faces turned upwards in agony, clawing the air with their last breath, as if trying to hang onto life itself.

Hannemann flashed them a last look as he began to veer to

the left, followed by the two sobbing officers, stumbling onwards with last of their strength. The Russians wouldn't last a minute more; then the survivors would go to ground and they would find themselves trapped between them and the second wave, some hundred metres behind them, in the whirling smoke and the deafening noise. They had to get on!

A group of fur-hatted infantrymen appeared out of nowhere, their weapons already lost, their eyes wild with fear. They had broken. They were running away. Hannemann didn't give them a chance to discover the Germans in their midst. With a grunt, he pulled the pin and flung the grenade in one and the same moment. It exploded with a soft plop. White smoke, thick and choking, started to pour from it instantly. The Russians disappeared from view. The three fugitives staggered on.

Thick white smoke was everywhere. They saw the machine-gunner crouched behind his old-fashioned Russian Maxim when it was too late. They recoiled. But the Russian sitting upright behind the tripod was minus his head. It lay in a puddle of congealed blood at his side, as if he might well have placed it there neatly so as not to get in the way. They ran on.

More Russians loomed up out of the smoke, split here and there by the glowing morse of tracer. Hannemann heaved his second grenade. They jumped back, thinking it was HE* and disappeared too in the sudden burst of blinding white smoke.

A Russian came reeling towards them, face black and bleeding from a nasty wound over his right eye. Hannemann's boot lashed out. The man screamed thinly and fell reeling to the shattered ground, clutching his ruined groin.

A bright red ball exploded suddenly to their left. The blast slapped them damply across their shocked faces. They gasped, as the very air was dragged out of their lungs. Hanno von Heiter staggered. For one horrified moment de la

*High explosive

Mazière saw him sway, glimpsed as if at the bottom of a murky trembling pool, knowing that if he were hit, he couldn't carry him to their own lines; he was too weak. 'You hit, Hanno?' he croaked.

'Don't think so . . . blast, I think,' Hanno said weakly, feeling the sudden hot wetness in his tunic, but not daring to look. 'Yes, I'll manage.'

'*Los!*' Hannemann urged. 'Not much farther now. Got to keep at it. . . . *Got to!*'

Like drunks, they stumbled on, falling to their knees, clawing their way up again, blinded by the smoke, tripped by the rusty barbed wire, adorned here and there with the bundles of wet rags which had once been men, knowing that if they stopped now, they would never move again.

They passed a group of Russian dead, sprawled out in a heap, arms flung about in abandon, the white hush of the tracer cutting through the smoke, painting their faces a strange hue. For some reason, which they couldn't comprehend, many of them were minus their feet.

A shell howled down, or perhaps it was a mortar bomb, to explode with a shattering roar fifty metres away, followed an instant later by another explosion—and another. For one long moment they stood there—it was impossible to run—buffeted by the blast, the shock wave plastering their rags to their skinny limbs, as the world rocked madly, the flesh flattened by the concussion. And then they saw it. Hannemann gasped. De la Mazière groaned weakly, '*Oh, not that!*' Hanno von Heiter began to blubber.

'*Achtung—Minen,*' the stencilled sign with its skull-and-crossbones warning read.

'*MINES—GERMAN MINES!*' The warning shot through Hannemann's brain. They had come so far and suffered so much danger and hardship, to be stopped at the very last moment by their own minefields. For an instant, the big tough NCO felt like breaking down himself and sobbing, too, like Hanno von Heiter, who had obviously reached breaking point. But he was seized by a great fiery rage at the injustice of it all. He grabbed Hanno von Heiter, filling his hand in something wet and warm and sticky. 'Stop it! For Chrissake, stop it!' With his free hand he slapped the officer across the face—hard.

The shock stopped Hanno. He stared white-faced and filthy at the big sergeant, eyes wet with tears and bulging with disbelief.

'Hannemann—' de la Mazière began weakly.

'You can fucking shoot me later, sir!' Hannemann cried, half crazed with rage and tension. 'But let's get through first.'

'Through?'

'Yes. Through the shitting minefield. Here, give me a hand with him.' He thrust Hanno von Heiter in front of him and hardly aware of what he was doing, Hanno allowed himself to be propelled forward, as the battlefield rocked and swayed under the German counter-barrage. A second later the other two followed, stepping over the wire which marked the zone of sudden death. They were in the minefield.

Sweating like pigs, the battle forgotten, the three men advanced at a snail's pace, hardly daring to breathe, each new step made only after what seemed an eternity of deliberation. Behind them the mortars plastered the Russian infantry and, in what seemed another world, they could hear the hoarse cries and curses of the enemy as they fell on all sides.

'*Mine!*' de la Mazière snapped suddenly, finding the danger had made his weariness vanish. Now he was a bundle of tingling nerves, eyes as keen as in the old days, roving back and forth restlessly, as they searched for that terrible threat.

They stopped as one. Together they stared at the little prong of wire protruding from the black earth. How harmless it looked! Yet beneath their feet it marked the spot where three or four pounds of explosive were buried: explosive which would rip their legs off, tear away their genitals, ruin them for life, turn them into crippled vegetables. Hannemann cursed and found he couldn't move. He had frozen. He had lost control of himself. He could hear his own harsh breathing and feel the cold trickle of sweat running down the small of his back. He had never experienced the intensity of his own body so much as at this moment.

But de la Mazière was now back in control. 'There's a pattern to them,' he announced confidently, not seeming to notice the obscene howl and thump of the mortar bombs still dropping into the billowing smoke. 'They're anti-tank mines facing the enemy. That's why, as you spotted, Hannemann, the Ivans no longer attacked in this area.'

He bent down and touched the prong gingerly. It didn't move under his touch. 'Yes, definitely anti-tank. Come on, we're quite safe.'

'But wouldn't they also lay anti-personnel,' Hanno von Heiter began in a voice that quavered and was badly out of control, clutching the silent bundle of Fifi to his sticky chest.

De la Mazière cut him short. 'Don't worry. I'll spot them soon enough. Follow me! There's too much iron in the air around here to suit me,' he attempted the old crack. The other two didn't laugh, but they tottered after him, eyes fixed on the ground, as if mesmerised.

An agonised eternity of five nerve-cracking minutes passed. Now they were leaving the mortar barrage behind them in the dense fog of war, which muted the cries of the Russians, and de la Mazière reasoned they were getting closer to their own lines. He also knew that if the stubble-hoppers defending the front had laid anti-personnel mines they should come across them soon.

As if on cue, Hannemann gasped, stumbling to a hurried halt. 'Sir, *look*!'

There was no mistaking the double-prong of an anti-personnel mine, set there to catch on an unwary Russian's boot, as he charged to death or mutilation.

'And over there, too, to the left,' Hannemann said in a frightened whisper.

De la Mazière shook off the paralysing fear which

threatened to overcome him once again. 'We've nothing to lift them with,' he said, controlling his voice with an effort of naked willpower, 'even if we knew how to. We've just got to go over them.'

'Detlev!'

De la Mazière did not hesitate. He lashed out and struck his old friend brutally across the face. It was the only way to put an end to his unreasoning panic. Hannemann caught the other officer as he reeled back, keeping his feet rooted to the spot where he stood. He was taking no chances.

As Hanno started to sob again like a broken-hearted child, de la Mazière, his voice like ice, snapped, 'I shall take the chances. I'm going ahead three metres. Hanno, you keep *exactly* in my footsteps. Understood?'

Hanno nodded his head brokenly.

'Hannemann, you bring up the rear, keeping in the Captain's exact path. Every few seconds, sing out. Perhaps the stubble-hoppers will hear us above this shitting racket. *Klar?*'

'*Klar!*' Hannemann replied with more confidence than he felt.

'Right, here we go!'

In a tense line they advanced, placing their feet gingerly as if on egg-shells, the only sound their own tense breathing and the muted rumble of the guns. To the rear, his voice parched and cracked, Hannemann cried, '*Nicht schiessen! Bitte nicht schiessen! wir sind Deutsche!*'* But there was no reply to his tense plea for recognition; for all they knew, there was no one to their front.

But there *was* to their rear.

'*Stoi?*' The harsh Russian challenge cut into their tensed bodies like a sharp knife.

Fur-hatted figures, carrying round-barrelled tommy-guns, began to appear through the fog and smoke.

---

*'Don't shoot. We are German.'

A machine pistol chattered. Tracer hissed through the air. A grenade exploded with a thick crump, only metres away. A mine exploded. Lethal silver balls sliced left and right. One of the Russians who had surprised them went down, his face disintegrating, splashing blood and gleaming white bone on all sides. '*Stoi?*' That angry cry rang out again, as yet more mines exploded and a squat, yellow-faced Russian, only metres away, was abruptly reduced to a dwarf, wedged on bloody stumps, staring fascinated at his own severed legs, dying as he crouched there.

De la Mazière hesitated no longer. It was the devil or the deep blue sea. '*Fuck the mines!*' he screamed above the high-pitched burr of the machine pistols and the angry cries in Russian. '*Run for it! It's our only chance! RUN!*' All around them, lead cut the air. Another mine exploded in a vivid flash of cruel, purple flame. Men screamed. A grenade whizzed at de la Mazière. He dodged it like a startled horse. The blast tossed him to one side. For one moment he knelt, sobbing for breath, eyes hardly taking in the two dead 'things' sprawled on the rusting wire, German or Russian, he did not know, headless and legless, looking like the offal butchers had once placed outside the doors to be picked up by the trash men before the war.

Hannemann grabbed him and heaved him to his feet. 'Come on, sir. We're nearly there!'.

'There!'

'German! They're calling over there in German!'

With the last of their strength, they pelted forward, leather-lunged and desperate, towards those grey, muddy figures rising from their holes like corpses from the grave, the blood dripping from Hanno von Heiter's dead bundle marking their progress over the ruined earth. *They had done it!*

PART THREE

Operation Citadel

CHAPTER 1

ALL THE Luftwaffe brass was there.

The great hall of the *Reichsluftschutzschule** at Gatow just outside Berlin was packed to the last seat with the men who in this fourth year of war commanded Germany's Air Force squadrons.

Greim, seated among his own officers, knowing that they stood out against the grey of the Luftwaffe in their black leather SS tunics, noted just how young the commanders had become. The men who had fought the early air battles of the war were no longer there, unless they had escaped the great slaughter by promotion to the staff. Now battle squadrons were commanded by men who had been sergeants in 1939 and the groups by former second-lieutenants who were now colonels.

Up front sat the heroes, handsome, young, highly decorated aces whose faces every German knew from the illustrated magazines and the picture postcards which were sold now, as if they bore the handsome mugs of pre-war UFA film stars. The General of Bomber Pilots, young, slim with a narrow fine-featured face. The General of Fighter Pilots beside him, moustachioed and virile, contrasting strongly with the other commander. Luetzow, Steinhoff, Wernicke, and all the rest of them who had survived the carnage of these long bitter years of war.

Greim smiled softly to himself. Once he and his young bloods of the SS who flew the Stukas would have been up there with the *prominenz*. But not now. 1943's heroes were the fighter pilots who went up daily above the hard-pressed Reich to tackle the flying 'furniture vans' of the RAF and the

*Imperial Air Defence School

8th US Air Force. Cannonbird or not, the Stuka and its pilots had fallen into obscurity.

Next to him Baron Karst, his second-in-command, seemed to have read his thoughts; for he said, gesturing angrily at the bemedalled, laughing young fighter pilots at the front of the big echoing hall, already passing silver flasks of cognac to one another (for mostly they were drunk when not on duty), 'Look at them, perfumed and pomaded like a bunch of warm brothers behind Lehrter Station! What a rotten bunch!' His hard face contorted scornfully. 'Thank God, we don't have that type in the SS Officer Corps.'

Greim shrugged and at his other side, von Einem, who had long grown cynical about the SS, the Luftwaffe, indeed about the whole war, winked at him and said, 'My dear Karst, what can you expect from chaps who did not have the privilege of being born into the right class like ourselves, what!'

Baron Karst screwed the monocle, which he affected (his vision was a perfect 20-20), more tightly into his eye and stared hard at the other SS officer, as if he did not quite know whether his leg was being pulled.

Von Einem looked serious and Karst concluded that the remark was not meant cynically. 'How right you are, my dear fellow,' he agreed. 'We have had dignity, bearing—and modesty bred into our very bones.'

There was a hasty scraping of chairs and shuffling of feet, as the senior general, the commander of the Imperial Air Fleet, sprang to his feet, hand raised in the Hitler salute.

There was Goering, dressed in a white uniform of his own design, the Blue Max at his throat, his chest glittering with rows of bejewelled decorations. He stood there, a look of scorn on his gross berouged face, and waited until the general had reported in the prescribed manner, 'Imperial Marshal, I beg to report that there is present . . .'

Greim let the words drone on, staring at the man who had been his first commander in the Old War and wondered what had happened to the lean young fighter ace he had known then. The mouth was still resolute, but over the years it had become sensual, the mouth of a *bon viveur*, perhaps even decadent.

But there was nothing soft or decadent about the gross Marshal's opening remarks. Without wasting any time on preliminaries, he launched straight into the attack. '*I have spoiled you!*' he bellowed, hands on his fat hips, red jowls wobbling in anger. 'Too many decorations, too many parties, too many women! Bomber pilots, fighter pilots, dive-bomber pilots—you have all become fat and lazy!'

There were gasps of astonishment and outrage throughout the hall. Some of the aces at the front, half rose to their feet to be hauled down again by their more self-contained comrades. At the back someone shouted in anger and a couple of pilots cried '*Pfui!*' Next to Greim, Baron Karst gripped his SS dagger-of-honour in a white-knuckled hand and hissed, 'The perfumed dog! He is maligning the honour of the Armed SS. *Reichsführer* Himmler will hear of this!'

Greim smiled softly to himself. He knew Goering of old. He was going to anger them before putting on the charm—it was the well-known 'Chink food tactic'—sweet and sour. He was leading them up to something, and he half-suspected what it might be.

'Every day the Anglo-American air gangsters and terrorists fly over our Imperial German territory with impunity,' Goering raved on, working himself up to a fine fury. 'But where are my fighters? *Where indeed?* Not a single one is to be seen. Where is our vaunted Luftwaffe, the civilians in our great cities are crying out? Where is our protection? Have we no defence against these flying criminals from America and England?' He dabbed his glistening brow and hastily took a swig from a silver flask of cognac offered him by one of his immaculate aides.

'Of course, my generals supply me with figures, *wonderful* figures of the number of Tommies and Amis shot down.' He looked scornfully at his senior commanders. 'They are just

one big damned lie! Do you think, in God's name, that
anyone in the civilian population believes those astronomical
figures. *Of course, they shittingly well don't!'* He snorted and took
another swig of the *kognak*. Now most of his listeners, especially
the fighter aces, who had a guilty conscience anyway at the
mass destruction of German cities, were staring down at their
feet, faces pale. 'We've made an almighty fool of ourselves, not
only in the eyes of our own poor people, but in the eyes of the
Anglo-Americans as well. You haven't made a fraction of the
kills you reported.'

Greim frowned. Fat Hermann was going too far, as he
stood up there, red with rage, shaking his red-painted finger
at them, that gross body wobbling disgustingly. He was
beginning to feel ashamed of his former commander.
How could he shame his fighter pilots thus in front of the
bomber, dive-bomber and transport pilots. What was he
after? Did he think his cynical indictment would fan the
flagging spirit of his outnumbered fighter pilots . . . fill them
with fresh dedication?

The vulgar gibes, the accusations, the threats went on and
on, with Fat Hermann pointing his quivering forefinger at his
stunned audience time and time again, calling them cowards,
liars, malingerers.

Slowly, however, the diatribe started to change. The 'sour'
part of the old 'Chink food tactic' began to give way to
'sweet'. Now Fat Hermann was throwing in a few glib phrases
to restore his audience's badly shaken confidence. 'Not saying
you're *all* cowards . . . there's many a noncom who's an
example to his officers, as I shall show you in due course.
Junior officers, too, imbued with the spirit of self-sacrifice of
Nationalism Socialism. . . . Eighteen year olds straight from
flying schools prepared to die if they can knock one of those
air gangsters out of the sky . . . death before dishonour. . . .
But they are the few, a very few. The time has come for *all*,' he
emphasised the words with a great sweeping gesture of his fat
arms and Greim could see the dark sweat patches at his

armpits, 'my pilots to show the same determination and bravery and spirit of self-sacrifice!' He reeled suddenly and felt for the table behind him, as if he suddenly needed its support.

Hurriedly a couple of his elegant adjutants rushed on to the stage and Greim told himself grimly he knew why: Fat Hermann needed another 'snort'. But it wasn't going to be cognac this time.

The senior general seized the opportunity presented him. He sprang to his feet, while Goering fumbled in his pocket and cried in one of those vulgar, emotional voices that all the 'golden pheasants' seemed to have cultivated in these last years, Greim couldn't help thinking cynically, '*Herr Reichsmarschall*, in this hour of darkness we are filled with an unswerving determination to fight on till final victory! We have taken your words to heart! We pledge unreservedly the last precious drop of our blood in the fight for Folk, Fatherland and Führer!'

No one took any notice of him. The eyes of the assembled pilots were fixed on their fat commander busily inserting the bejewelled tube up his nose through which he would sniff his dose of cocaine, or still on their gleaming boots, as if they could not shake off their mood of despair and shame. A few, Greim noted sadly, were openly crying. Goering had gone too far.

Fat Hermann did not seem to notice when he took up his stance once more, eyes gleaming, face flushed with sparkling new, drug-induced energy. 'So, comrades,' he commenced in his old style, 'I've had you with your hooters deep in the crap—and, believe me, you deserved it, some of you. Now, let's hear the good news, eh?' He ripped at his collar, as if it were too tight for him and beamed at them, the very essence of the jovial fat man who hadn't a care in the world. Greim sighed. If nothing else, his old squadron commander was a decided card. He waited for what was to come.

'Comrades!' Goering leaned forward, the sweat glistening

on his moonlike face. 'In the East we are going over to the offensive again. We're going to knock those damned piss pansies of Popovs right out of the war! Once and for all. And,' he raised his forefinger high, 'we of the Luftwaffe, fighters, bombers, dive-bombers, are going to play a very, very significant part in that last battle in the East.'

An excited murmur ran through the crowded assembly. Next to Greim, Baron Karst's eyes gleamed fanatically and he whispered. 'I knew it. I knew it all the time—the Führer, in his infinite wisdom, *did* have something up his sleeve! Back there on the Dnieper, it was all a strategic withdrawal to suck the Russians into a trap.' He flashed a bold, aggressive glance at Greim. 'That's the reason for the cannonbird, sir. We are going over to the offensive once more.'

Greim did not reply. He couldn't. His mind was racing. So his little 'canary' in Berlin had been right after all. The balloon was soon to go up once more in Russia.

Goering raised his pudgy hands for silence. 'Comrades, comrades!' he cried in his most vibrant and winning voice. 'Let me explain. This month our brave soldiers in the East have finally managed to stabilise the front. But the winter fighting has left two mutually jutting salients. A German, centred at the town of Orel, jutting eastwards. And a Russian, jutting westwards around the industrial city of Kursk.'

'Now, comrades, even to someone like myself who would never have qualified for the purple stripe—'Goering meant that of the staff officer—'even if he had gone to the shitting staff college for an eternity, that means we have the making of two rival pincer movements. One that the Popovs could execute at Orel—and one that we could carry out from the north and south to cut off the Kursk salient and all the Russian forces within it. It is that which the Führer, in his great wisdom and infinite foresight, has decided on.'

This time carried away by his own drug-induced excitement, Goering did not give them an opportunity to absorb

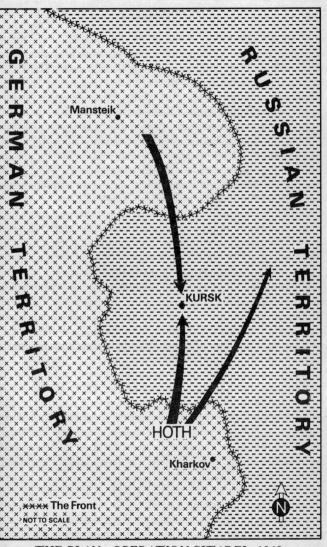

GERMAN TERRITORY

RUSSIAN TERRITORY

Mansteik

KURSK

HOTH

Kharkov

×××× The Front
NOT TO SCALE

N

THE PLAN—OPERATION CITADEL, 1943.

the tremendous news. Instead he hurried on, the words tripping from his tongue, his fat chest heaving with the effort of so much rapid talking. 'Stalingrad last year rallied the German Folk behind the Führer. Just as Dunkirk placed the decadent, treacherous English behind that drunken Jewish sot, Churchill, Stalingrad has done the same for our beloved Führer. Since January the men and women comrades of Germany's war industry have worked all out, fourteen . . . *eighteen* hours a day to put new weapons, vehicles, planes everything in the hands of their comdrades at the front. Now the Führer has built up the greatest force ever assembled by the *Wehrmacht*. Two huge armies of fifty divisions, sixteen of them armoured. They contained nine hundred thousand men armed with ten thousand guns and with three thousand tanks. Never in the whole history of war has such a tremendous striking force in man and material been created! There will be another twenty divisions in reserve . . .'

On and on, Goering went, without once referring to his notes, reeling off one startling statistic after another, while his audience stared up at his fat sweating bulk, their mood changing from sullen despair to disbelief, bewilderment, confusion, and on to glowing, exhilarated enthusiasm, their faces suddenly animated with new energy . . . hope.

It was a tremendous performance, Greim told himself, tensed and waiting for the role of the Luftwaffe and, in particular, that of the 1st SS Stuka Group. Even 'old hares' such as himself and von Einem were impressed. He could see that all right. In a minute, Goering would have his audience on its feet, cheering and saluting as in the good, old days; and even as he waited, Greim mused whether it was still possible. *Could Germany still win?*

'*Should* Germany win?' the harsh little voice at the back of his mind taunted him abruptly.

Greim frowned, the excited throng all around him, forgotten suddenly. He had seen the results of the RAF and 8th USAF raids on Germany's great cities. They had been terror raids, there was no doubt about that. The Anglo-Americans made no distinction between civilian and military targets. Perhaps they were not capable of the same pin-pointing bombing that Stuka pilots could carry out. But that wasn't important. Weren't the Anglo-Americans just reacting to the initial terror that the Third Reich had inflicted on Europe? Would not—*should* not—Germany be punished for what the Fatherland had done in Russia, in the end?

'Now then, comrades,' Goering was saying, his voice now growing hoarse with so much ranting, 'you will be asking yourselves what part we of the Luftwaffe will be playing in this great Operation Citadel at Kursk?' Greim forgot his doubts. He tensed. Whatever the right or wrong of Germany's cause, he knew he had a duty to save his young bloods of the SS and their Luftwaffe air-gunners, come what may. He waited.

'A tremendous one!' Goering boomed, answering his own question. 'Perhaps the most important role of all in the initial stages of the operation. I am making seventeen hundred planes available for the first days of the attack. One thousand bombers, fighters, ground-attack and anti-tank planes under the command of General Seidemann here will support the attack of the 4th Panzer Army under General Hoth from the south in the Byelgorod region. The remaining seven hundred . . .'

Greim was no longer listening. So that was it! His cannonbirds would be supporting Hoth's Fourth Panzer. He frowned. That meant frontline tank-busting ops. But what about Ivan fighters? They'd be there in their hundreds once the Ivans realised that this was a major op. Not even the new cannonbird would be much good against massed enemy fighters, working in close co-operation with the Ivan ground defenders.

Goering seemed able to read his mind and that of the other Stuka commanders, for Greim heard him saying, 'Now, I know you comrades of the Stuka squadrons have felt you have been neglected in these past years, flying a plane that was under-armoured and under-powered. Now you've got your tank-buster—the cannonbird. All the same, you are asking yourselves, who is going to give you the protection you need while you are about your job of knocking out the Ivan armour?' He beamed at the men in the back row, shouting out a few names of those he recognised, his gaze falling on Greim, 'Well, I tell you, Walter, you old sauce-hound—with that ugly mug of yours.'

There was a ripple of laughter at the pleasantry and Greim smiled, too, in no way offended at the Reichmarshal's reference to his terribly scarred face. It was all part of Goering's game. He had them, all of them, eating out of his fat hand now. He could do with them what he wished, as he had done once back in the great days when he had summoned them from throughout the world where they been living in virtual exile, as he, himself, had been doing, to create the greatest air force the world had ever seen.

'This time the Stuka is not flying unescorted. *No sir!*' Goering was emphatic, his jowls wobbling. 'Every single cannonbird squadron will be covered by a fighter one. Not only that, our long-range bomber squadrons will go straight for the Ivan fighter fields in the very first hour of the great offensive. Yes,' he declared proudly, throwing out his massive chest. 'This time we will slaughter the Russian fighters on the ground. So don't worry, Walter, this time you and your Stuka boys won't have to piss yer pants. We'll hand-carry you to the Ivan armour and powder yer bottom with talcum powder while you knock 'em off, as easily as if you were at a peacetime shooting gallery.' He waved a hand at Greim and then dismissed him in the gale of laughter that greeted his remarks. He snapped his fingers urgently and stood there like a white hippo, face red and sweat-glazed, the eyes still sparkling feverishly, but the smile gone from his painted lips.

A moment later the adjutant returned and whispered something in Goering's ear. The latter nodded and raised his hands for silence. 'Comrades, before you are dismissed, I have one last word to say to you. I will not appeal to your patriotism. Nor to your devotion to duty, courage and all the rest of the big words. I shall leave all that to finer orators than I.' He paused and they waited, as the adjutant turned to the man waiting in the wings like an actor eager for his call.

'We are not fighting human beings there in the East, comrades,' Goering continued, voice without emotion, suddenly monotonous. 'Two months ago those savages called Russians masquerading as humans fell on one of our bases. Only three men survived to tell us the terrible things that happened there that day. Two were officers who are currently receiving hospital treatment in Berlin. One is sufficiently recovered—a humble NCO—to come here now and tell you exactly what this new battle is being fought for—to stop what happened there happening in our own beloved country.' He extended his right hand like a compère introducing the star of the evening. Slowly, very slowly, supported by a stick which he handled with difficulty, a terribly skinny Luftwaffe man in a plain grey tunic devoid of badges of rank and decoration, save for the black and white of the Knight's Cross at his throat, started to hobble into the circle of bright white light.

Greim gasped as if he had just seen a ghost and at his side, Baron Karst whispered, 'In three devils' name! It's . . . *Sergeant Hannemann*!'

CHAPTER 2

MAJOR DE LA Mazière walked slowly down the East-West Axis, enjoying the brisk Berlin morning, the sense of bustle and activity all around, as the workers streamed to their offices and war factories, automatically saluting the men in field-grey and ignoring the looks of admiration thrown at him by the girls in their turbans and thin, white, springtime *Staubmäntel**.

He had been on convalescent leave for a month, now, ever since he, Hanno, and Hannemann had staggered into their own lines and collapsed, to wake up twenty-four hours later in a long ambulance train chugging its way through Poland on the way to the Reich. Now he was an out patient at the capital's famed *La Charité* hospital, together with Hanno, both of them sent there personally by *Reichsführer SS* Heinrich Himmler—'my brave Stuka pilots *must* have the best treatment available in the whole of the Reich!'

Hannemann was around somewhere. He had recovered more quickly than his two officers and, after his top-secret visit to Gatow, he had been released to his own home in Berlin and was very probably taking his own form of convalescence —in the shape of beer, bed, and broads. De la Mazière grinned to himself, his skinny face still bearing the strain of the terrible ordeal in the wilds of Russia.

This fine morning at nine sharp, the three of them would meet again to be examined perfunctorily by *Oberstabsarzt* Professor Kroeger, a genial, fat-bellied professor of medicine masquerading as a military doctor, who would invariably clap them on their skinny shoulders, saying, 'Yes, another month free of military duties, I'd say, what, my boys? I think

*Literally 'dust-coats', a kind of thin white raincoat

the Greater German Wehrmacht will survive a further four weeks without you.' De la Mazière frowned. He knew from Hannemann that the 1st SS Stuka Group was already in the process of moving back to the Eastern Front to take part in some tremendous new op. there. If he accepted Kroeger's kindness—for it was just that; all of them were really fit for flying duties again—he would miss whatever the High Command had planned for them over there.

The tall, harshly handsome Major paused under one of the fine trees hung with camouflage nets; the whole broad avenue that ran straight through Berlin was hung with netting so that it didn't offer a landmark for the enemy bombers which came day and night these days. From one of the great lumbering double-decker buses, hung with the usual wartime slogans, a group of giggling factory girls waved at him. Automatically, hardly aware of the hero-worship in their eyes, he waved back.

Did he want another month of leave in the Reich? he asked himself. It was a question that had plagued him for a week or more now ever since he had visited his grey-haired father, the General, in his East Prussian estate.

The last night at home in that great, echoing, tumbledown house that smelled of stale cabbage and animal manure; for the old man no longer had the money to keep on the small army of servants which had once maintained the place, his father had suddenly snorted, 'Detlev, how much longer are you going to hang around Berlin like some wretched rear-echelon stallion, making love to loose women and drinking far too much?' He had tugged at his ragged ex-cavalryman's moustache and rocked back and forth on the saddle which he affected as a chair. 'Not the sort of thing one expects of a de la Mazière, you know, old chap.' He had indicated the gloomy panelled study, hung with the fading flags and yellowing trophies of generations of service to the Prussian and Imperial Armies. 'Never had any of those sort of Johnnies in our family. In wartime the place of a de la Mazière is at the front, even if you are flying one of those things of yours!'

De la Mazière had smiled, but his eyes had not lit up. His father had always seen things in black and white. If Germany fought, then the de la Mazières fought, too. Why they fought and against whom was no concern of the de la Mazières. 'Is it as simple as you, perhaps, see it, sir?' he had ventured hesitantly.

The General had glowered at him under his bushy eyebrows, while outside the peasants sang wearily, some of them in Polish, for this was close to the border, as they wended their way home to the estate cottages. 'And what is that supposed to mean, sir?'

De la Mazière had cleared his throat carefully and had dearly hoped the old man would offer him a glass of that fiery local *Korn* which he guarded so jealously; schnaps was getting very difficult to get on the open market. Now, even in the provinces, there were two 'alcohol-free days' a week. 'Sir, you may not know it, but there is a tragedy in the making over there—in Russia.'

'*Tragedy?*'

'Yes sir. We seem to be holding our own again. Perhaps from what I have heard in Berlin, we are ready to go over to the offensive again. But what purpose will it serve?'

'What do you mean, my boy? *What purpose will it serve?*'

'For me, sir, it would be a kind of revenge to go back there. I have seen some terrible things in Russia, sir, which I would dearly like to pay back.' De la Mazière had shaken his head, as the events of that field flashed through his mind's eye once more—the raped kitchen-women, the crucified priest, the mutilated bodies of the crewmen. 'But in the end where would it all lead? The lives of our brave young men would be thrown away for,' he had shrugged a little helplessly, finding it difficult to formulate his confused thoughts about Russia, 'for those damned golden pheasants who have battened on the Russians in the rear areas and turned them against us!

With their greed, their cruelty, their skirt-chasing, their sheer common vulgarity, those fat brown-shirted Party bosses are losing the war for us out there. *So why fight on?*' He had paused, skinny chest heaving with the effort.

For a long while there had been silence in the old house, broken only by the steady tick of the grandfather clock in the dark hall outside.

'I understand, Detlev,' his father had said finally, his voice weary and without hope. 'The old virtues and traditions are dead. We have been swamped by the brown vulgarity of—er—those golden pheasants, as you call them. They are little men, you know, Detlev, burdened by the little man's concept of grandeur.' He had favoured his son with a weak smile, the fierce light gone from his eyes for a moment and in that instant, de la Mazière had realised, with the absolute clarity of a vision, that he would never see his father again; the old man would die soon. 'But my boy, we de la Mazières have never concerned ourselves with the politics and antics of little men, ever since the first de la Mazière fled from the mob in France and offered his services to the King of Prussia.' His father's voice had hardened. 'Detlev, you do *not* serve the little men, *you serve Germany*!' The words were said without emotion, without any appeal, but simply as a matter of fact. 'That is what the de la Mazières have always done—*served Germany*!'

Another heavy silence had descended upon the house, as the General froze in his saddle, suddenly old and deflated, as the rooks in the tall oaks of the drive cawed and the clock ticked away time with metallic inexorability.

For a while Detlev stared around that dark room, heavy with the memories of the de la Mazières who had come here at the end of their days on battlefields all over Europe, simply to die, just as his father, the General, would do. But that room gave no hope, no confidence, no belief in the continuity of things—from past, present, to the future—as it had once done. Even now he knew he would never have a son to pass on what he knew of his ancestors. Instinctively, he knew that all this would vanish one day, *and one day soon*, when the red tide swamped this eastern-most province which had been German for a thousand years ever since the Black Knights had wrest it from the grasp of the Slavs. 'They' were coming back and there was nothing he, a twentieth-century black knight who rode a plane instead of a horse, could do to stop them.

'Well?' the General had barked with a trace of his old authority, 'What is it going to be, Detlev?'

But all Detlev de la Mazière had been able to stammer was an uncertain, 'I'm afraid, I don't quite know, sir. . . .' The old man had not come to the door to see him off the next morning as Frantek, the coachman, had brought the tired old nag round to the front of the house to take him back to the station for the train to Berlin; but Detlev de la Mazière had caught one last glimpse of him through the study window: a bowed old man, slumped in his silly saddle, surrounded by the battered mementoes of two centuries of tradition and service to the state, his fine white head bent as if in defeat. In the dark coach, safe from prying eyes, as the peasants took off their caps and their kerchiefed womenfolk had curtsied in respect, he had wept for the very first time since he had been a schoolboy. He would never come home again. Now he started to walk again, listening to the first faint wail of the sirens to the west indicating yet another raid on the capital, and wondered what he should do.

Sergeant Hannemann wondered too, as he came to at last in the dirty crumpled bed, with the naked whore leaning over him, her face strained and tired and yet concerned as she held the ice-cold beer up for him to drink. 'Thought you might like this after last night.'

Hannemann blew off the froth and took a deep grateful drink. 'Thanks,' he said thickly, 'just like mother's milk!' He

eyed the whore's hanging breasts, as he said the words, but
without sexual interest, all energy spent now.

'You said, you have to report for a medical this morning,'
she said, slipping on a cheap artificial silk gown. 'Thought I'd
better wake you in time.'

Hannemann drank the beer happily, taking in the dirty
little room with its damp patches and holed black-out
curtains, now drawn back to let in the bright morning light.
'Yes, just routine. The old bone-mender—he's some sort of
professor or other—will give us another month, I'm sure of
that. I've got him a box of lung torpedoes from the black
market and a half-kilo of real bean coffee. That should do the
trick, I shouldn't be surprised.'

She nodded encouragingly and, flipping of the screw cap,
poured more beer into the chipped mug with the old picture
of some urchin urinating into a puddle, above the legend,
'*NEVER DRINK WATER!*'

He smiled and accepted it gratefully. 'That's right enough.
They say—*fishes fuck in water!*' he agreed. 'Give me suds and
sauce any day. Nice night,' he said after a moment,
remembering her clad only in a black corset and sheer silk
stockings rolling around the bed in ecstasy, faked or
otherwise, he didn't know or care, giving him a real old
mattress polka. 'The marie* is under yer pillow.'

'Thank you. More beer, soldier?'

'No. Just hand me me dice-beakers and uniform. My
officers will be waiting for me at *La Charité*.'

Obediently she handed him his gleaming boots and
uniform, as he struggled into his underpants and socks,
stroking the tunic free of creases as she waited to give it to him.
'You've been around, I see,' she said, indicating the heavily
bemedalled front of the jacket. 'All that tin. Narvik
Medal . . . Crete. North Africa . . . Iron Cross, first and
second class—and oh, you've cured your throat ache too, I

*Slang for 'money'

see!' she said a little surprised, as he hung the black and white ribbon of the Knight's Cross around his brawny throat before taking the tunic.

'You know your medals?'

'It's my profession,' she answered with a bored smile. 'The tin tells you a lot about the field-greys. I mean some of those stubble-hoppers, the real old, hairy-assed old hares from Popovland, can be pretty mean to a working girl after a couple of years out there without a woman.'

'Spect they can,' Hannemann answered without much interest. Ever since he had been able to stir up the old salami to something approaching a real diamond-cutter, he'd had a different whore a night. He didn't know why. All he knew was that he wanted to pack in as much experience as possible in the time left to him. This one had been good, but already he was forgetting her. Tonight, God willing, he'd have another pavement-pounder, perhaps a blonde. 'You're not from Berlin,' he said, beginning to knot his tie. 'Tell from the accent.'

'Booty German,'* she answered. 'West Prussian.'

'Polack?'

'Sort of. Water-Polacks they used to call us back home, half Polish, half German.'

He nodded and reached for his cap, setting it on the side of his cropped head in a suitably rakish angle, patting it till it sat correctly.

The whore's eyes narrowed when she saw the black and white armband on his right sleeve, with its proud legend '*SS STUKA GESCHWADER*'. 'But you're not SS,' she said. '*You're Luftwaffe!*' Behind his back, her dark eyes set in those big slanting Slavic cheekbones gleamed unseen. Now she was no longer the tolerant, easy-going whore of a minute before.

'First SS,' he said, still looking at his reflection in the fly-blown mirror. 'The SS gents fly 'em. We common swine of the

*Name given to ethnic Germans incorporated in the Reich through conquest

Luftwaffe—peasants we call ourselves—fight 'em as air-gunners,' he explained without much interest.

'I see. I've heard of you. Once you were always in the papers. "The Führer's flying artillery", they used to call you. Always where there was a hot spot at the front. Suppose you'll be going back to Popovland soon?'

Hannemann chuckled. '*Not* Mrs Hannemann's handsome son, my little cheetah, well not this day at least. The rest of them.' He shrugged carelessly. 'They're already rolling eastwards—and half the shitting Luftwaffe with them. It's going to—' There was an urgent honking of a car horn outside. He straightened up suddenly, and reached for his well-polished belt. 'Hey, girlie, cast a glassy orb outside and see if there's a posh-looking officer-and-gent sitting out there in a fancy sports car, willya?'

She nodded and started unscrewing the catch, while Hannemann hurriedly completed his toilet. Hanno von Heiter had dropped him off at this place the night before after they had got drunk enough to want to dance an urgent mattress polka. Perhaps he had remembered and wanted to take him to the *la Charité*? The whore looked down at the long elegant, pre-war sports car and its driver in the black of the SS, hunched over the wheel, staring into nothing, as he pressed the horn at regular intervals. 'Yes,' she called, 'it's an SS—' Just in time she caught herself from calling him 'swine', as was her custom when talking to the rest of her 'cell' about the Black Guards.

'Thanks, girlie,' Hannemann said airily and marched to the door. 'See you sometime. Don't give anybody any free rides.'

'See you,' she agreed heartily and smiled at the old crack. 'That I won't, Sergeant! *Tschüss!*'

'*Tschüss*,' Hannemann said and with that he was gone out of her life, another of the score of men who slept with her for money each week.

Her smile vanished immediately to be replaced by a

thoughtful frown. Was it worth reporting to 'Anton', the cunning-eyed head of their 'cell', who worked as road-sweeper like so many other 'water-Polacks'? He said he was one of them, a simple farmboy from the Graudenz area who had been recruited back in '41 for work in the Reich, lured there as so many *Ostarbeiter** had been by the promise of good food and money—and the unspoken threat of the 'camps' if they didn't 'volunteer'. But she didn't believe him. He was no 'simple farmboy'. She thought of the handsome young officer in his big car with the Mark of Cain on him—the silver death's head of the Black Guards—and made up her mind. She would tell Anton what the big noncom had told her. Who knows—it might be good for a screw of that white powder, that blessed powder without which she could no longer live these days. She started to dress.

'How did it go, sir?' Hannemann asked happily, as Hanno steered the car into the throng of coal-driven buses and horse-drawn carts, honking his horn imperiously every time someone threatened to get in his way.

'Shitting awful!' Hanno von Heiter answered miserably. 'I thought last night, I was going to do it. The champus, I thought, would do the trick.' He shook his head and narrowly missed running over a fat air raid warden on an ancient bike, pedalling all-out to reach his post before the bombs started.

'No diamond cutter?' Hannemann asked sympathetically.

'*Diamond-cutter*,' Hanno snorted. 'Not even a damned mild blue-veiner.' He shook his head. 'Frankly, Hannemann, I think I've had it. I'm shittingly well impotent!'

'Never say die, sir,' Hannemann urged, as von Heiter weaved in and out of the slow-moving morning traffic, as the sirens sounding the alarm moved ever closer from the west of the great city. Here and there, civilians stalled at the lights

*East Workers, i.e. labourers recruited in the occupied territories to the east

were looking up at the sky anxiously, and out of the corner of his eye, Hannemann noted a fat middle-aged policeman hiding behind a kiosk, quietly slipping on his steel helmet. There was undoubtedly trouble to come.

'Die, that's the only word for it,' von Heiter said gloomily. 'Ever since I lost poor little Fifi, what bit of luck I once had has vanished. Now I can't even get a diamond-cutter.'

'Strain, sir, under-nourishment, you know what the bone-mender said,' Hannemann tried to console him. 'Besides, sir, we're alive, aren't we? Alive, and not in Popovland, but right here, home with mother!'

Von Heiter took his gaze off the road for a moment. To the west now, the sky was peppered with silent exploding balls of dark-brown flak. The Amis were on their way, Hannemann thought, as the pale-faced young officer stared at him with eyes that no longer showed fear, as in the old days, but simply reflected his fatalism. 'Alive, did you say, Hannemann?'

The sergeant nodded.

'But for what—and for how long?'

Hannemann shrugged eloquently. 'Am I Jesus, sir? I start walking across the water next week.'

He forced a smile, telling himself that once he had hated the young aristocrat with his haughty, arrogant ways; now his hate had vanished and all he could feel was a kind of rough sympathy. Hanno von Heiter had death written all over him. He wasn't a survivor like Mrs Hannemann's handsome son, no sir. 'What's the use of thinking about tomorrow in our line of business, sir,' he said, his voice softer now, as the first low rumbling of artillery started to waft their way and people were already beginning to queue at the entrances of the towering concrete air-raid shelters, while the wardens fumbled with the keys to let them in. 'It's best to live for the day, don't you think?'

'But if the day brings nothing, Hannemann?' von Heiter countered. 'What then? What is there to live for then, tell me that, will you?'

But before Hannemann could attempt to answer that overwhelming question, the sirens on the post office to their right began to sound their shrill, nerve-chilling warning. Abruptly there were helmeted wardens everywhere, blowing their whistles, twirling their rattles, bellowing orders. The traffic slowed to a halt. Von Heiter braked, as to their left in the park, the flak guns thundered and above them, as if by magic, the blue sky was packed with a solid mass of silver birds, squadron after squadron of them, trailing white vapour after them, zooming in for the kill . . .

CHAPTER 3

THE SIRENS sounded the 'all clear'. But as the bewildered citizens emerged from their shelters, Berlin's agony continued. Even as the three of them came up with the rest of the shabby civilians, they could smell the sweet, nauseating stench of burning flesh. For the silver birds, the slaughter now complete, turning westwards, had done their work well. First they had saturated the city with phosphorus bombs and followed them with high explosive to spread the flames by the blast. Now the capital was being inexorably eaten up, by those greedy bright white flames.

Shielding his eyes against that incandescent glare, as all around them the tall buildings swayed and trembled like blazing stage backdrops, de la Mazière tried to orientate himself, while the other two stared open-mouthed at the terrible landscape transformed about them. All was panic-stricken movement. Streams of refugees fled past the three airmen, heading for the suburbs, bearing their pathetic bundles on their heads. A naked woman ran by screaming, the bright white pellets of phosphorus imbedded in both breasts already beginning to smoke again. She was soaked to the skin. Obviously she had thrown water over her naked body to stop the flames. Soon, however, now that the phosphorus had oxygen once more, it would begin to burn again, eating the flesh cruelly from her living body. A moment later she was followed by a bunch of terrified amputees hopping along as best they could in their blue and white hospital pyjamas, towing behind them, by means of belts, their war-blinded comrades, tears of fright trickling from unseeing eyes.

'Oh, my God, you can't believe it possible!' Hanno choked. 'Man couldn't do this to man. No!'

'Yes, he could, sir,' Hannemann answered, unusually grim. 'And worse. Look at that, sir.' He grabbed the young officer's skinny shoulder and turned him round by force.

Hanno von Heiter gasped. Next to a shattered building which bore the name '*Luth-Evang. Kindergarten*'*, the skeletal trees were filled with bits and pieces of what looked like pulped, over-ripe fruit from which dripped steadily a fig-red juice. Hanno vomited suddenly, the hot bile flooding through his tightly clenched fingers. Hanging there like ripe fruit were the shattered remains of little human bodies: the children from the nursery hurled into the stripped branches by the force of the blast!

De la Mazière fought back his nausea. 'Enough of these horrors!', he snapped, beginning to tremble all over, knowing that he would start to scream at any moment if he did not control himself. 'I think *la Charité* is somewhere in that direction. 'He pointed down the smoke-filled street, littered with the bodies of the dead, lying like bundles of abandoned rags. 'Come on, the two of you, let's get away from this!'

But there was no getting away from the horrors of the great city. They were everywhere, as the buildings to left and right crackled and burned merrily, and panic-stricken civilians ran to and fro, calling out the names of their loved ones. The dead lay everywhere, sprawled in the extravagant postures of the violently killed. Others crouched trembling in the water-tanks, noses barely above the surface, pleading for help, their bodies full of phosphorous pellets, waiting for the doctors to come and remove them, fearful to make the slightest move in case they burst into flames once more. A naked granny, dead, a charred baby clutched to ancient dugs which hadn't given milk these fifty years. A whore, legs spread to reveal the secret flesh below, as if in invitation, save that she was minus her head. A little white dog softly licking the face of a little girl,

*Protestant kindergarten

who looked as if she were asleep, whimpering pathetically. A fat middle-aged policeman, complete with leather *shako* and full uniform, blowing his whistle furiously, while he tried to balance on two bloody stumps. A car, its motor still running, with at its wheel, a completely naked man, save for a steel helmet, his body charred black and shrunken to the size of a pygmy by the tremendous heat. Horror after horror. There seemed no end to them as the three comrades crunched across the carpet of broken glass towards the hospital, their gazes fixed on the road, almost as if they were ashamed.

When they were about 200 metres from the nineteenth-century building of *la Charité*, its front and roof draped with huge red cross flags, they spotted them.

There were two of them heavily clad in fur-lined leather jackets and trousers, clumping along awkwardly in their thick flying suits, the one still carrying the bundle of his parachute cradled in his arms like a precious child. Behind them came their escort: two fat *Schupos*, their revolvers drawn, as if their prisoners might attempt to escape at any moment. All around women and children, faces contorted with hatred, raised their fists, cursed, spat upon the men in leather. But the latter seemed too weary to care, or perhaps they expected this kind of treatment. They plodded on towards their prison blindly, almost happily, taking no notice of the angry mob.

'Amis,' Hanno von Heiter said, and stopped as the little procession came towards them across the shattered cratered street. 'Ami flyers!'

'Shitting killers!' Hannemann cried thickly, clenching his fists, his broad face suddenly crimson with anger. 'Murdering women and little kids like that from seven or eight thousand metres!' He hawked and spat fiercely with contempt.

'Hold your water, Sergeant!' de la Mazière snapped and stared at the first two Americans he had ever seen in his life, as they got ever closer, the two policemen already straightening their shoulders at the sight of the two SS officers.

The one with the parachute was tall and burly with

gleaming white teeth. Even now as a prisoner, he had a kind
of swagger about him. De la Mazière guessed he would be his
squadron's most famous swordsman, a great success with the
ladies and fond of boasting of his conquests in the mess. The
other was smaller, swarthy, Italian in appearance and he
didn't look a day over eighteen.

Suddenly the swordsman spotted the three of them. He
whispered to his companion and smiled abruptly. 'Hi,' he
said and nodded at their wings, 'you guys flyers as well, eh?'
His smile broadened across his handsome, oil-begrimed face
and for one moment de la Mazière, possessed by a terrible icy
rage, thought he was going to shoot out his big hand to make
shakehands as the Amis called it. '*Flieger auch?*' he added to
make sure that he had been understood.

'Who are these men?' de la Mazière snapped to the bigger
of the policemen, whose chest bore the ribbons of the Old
War.

The policeman snapped to attention. 'Prisoners, American,
sir,' he barked, as if he were on a parade ground. 'Bomber
crashed in the Zoo region. These two only survivors.'

'Yeah,' the swordsman drawled, as if he had understood
the fat cop. 'We got lucky this time, didn't we, Rossi?'

The little Italian nodded dutifully, his dark liquid eyes
suddenly wary.

'*Kill them! String them up! They murder the innocent! Air
gangsters, cut the eggs off'n them with a blunt knife! Kill 'em!*' The
mob shrieked with rage, shaking their fists and spitting at the
two Americans. A woman ripped down her knickers to reveal
a fat wrinkled hairy belly and squatted next to the
swordsman, as if she were about to urinate on him.

Hastily the other cop pushed her aside and bellowed above
the racket. 'Now none of that! Get about your business. Make
feet I say! These are our prisoners. *Wirds bald?*'

De la Mazière held up his hand for silence and instinctively,
almost as if they knew that something dramatic was about to
happen, the crowd ceased shouting. His face suddenly

worried, the bigger of the two *Schupos* looked at the tall harshly handsome SS officer.

De la Mazière took his time, his eyes burning with sudden icy rage, gaze fixed on the unworried features of the swordsman, while behind them Hannemann muttered to himself, 'Don't deserve to be allowed to sit on their fat Ami arses for the rest of the war in some ritzy POW camp, with Red Cross parcels and shitting language courses and all the rest of it.' De la Mazière spoke, voice barely under control. 'We are taking over the Americans, *Herr Wachtmeister*,' he announced and took a step forward.

'But you can't do that, sir!' the other protested, while the throng leaned forward, eyes glittering feverishly. 'They are our prisoners and the law says—'

He stopped short. The SS officer's hand had dropped to the little pistol holster at his hip. '*This* is the law in 1943, *Herr Wachtmeister*,' he said harshly.

The swordsman looked puzzled, but managed to hide his uncertainty, big smile glued to his handsome face, as if he knew that nothing, *but nothing*, could ever happen to him. Wasn't he from God's Own Country after all? 'Hey, now what is this, guys?' he began. 'You want to take us to your mess or some—'

His words ended in a yelp of pain, as de la Mazière lashed out and slapped him open-handed across his face.

At his side, the Italian-looking one suddenly grew fearful. 'Knock it off, Bo! There's gonna be trouble.'

De la Mazière turned to the still muttering Hannemann. 'March them off behind that building, Sergeant!'

'Sir!' The big Berliner whipped out his pistol and rammed it hard into the side of the swordsman. 'All right, pretty boy,' he hissed, 'you heard the officer. March! You, too, nigger!' The Italian gulped hard and looked appealingly at his comrade, but the swordsman still holding his crimson face was already beginning to walk in the direction Hannemann indicated. De la Mazière nodded his satisfaction and turned back to the two bewildered policemen. 'Keep the civilians back, *Wachtmeister*,' he ordered. 'Hanno, you watch them.'

'But you can't do . . . what you're going to do, sir!' the bigger cop protested. 'It's—'

'You do it, sir,' the woman who had wanted to urinate on the American butted in. 'That's what the Amis bastards deserve. A bullet in the balls! If I had my way, I cut off their cocks with a blunt razorblade—*slowly*!' She held up one hand, as if dangling a sausage and with the other made cutting gestures, as if slicing a salami. The bigger policeman shuddered violently and looked abruptly at his big boots, as if ashamed.

De la Mazière dismissed them, eyes seeing nothing, but the leather-clad backs of the two Americans disappearing behind the shattered building. He followed Hannemann.

Numbly the crowd waited, their anger vanished. Even the woman was silent. Hanno waited too, shoulders hunched and tensed, as if he had half expected a blow. There was no sound save the heavy breathing of the cops, an ambulance siren far away, the steady crackle of flames. Time seemed to pass leadenly. All was silent behind the building.

Hanno jumped abruptly. A sudden wail—inhuman, eerie, like that of a desperate, trapped animal—broke the heavy brooding silence. 'No,' a broken voice shrieked hysterically, '*NO—PLEASE! PLEASE, DON'T*—'

The harsh dry crack of a pistol drowned the rest of that frantic plea for mercy. A second later it was followed by another. There was a dull moan and the slither of something slumping to the wrecked debris.

It took what seemed an age for Hannemann and de la Mazière to appear and when they did so, the fury had gone from their faces, as had that wild, glittering look in their eyes. They came back, shoulders slumped, drained, stumbling a little, faces suddenly bewildered, as if they could not quite realise themselves what they had just done.

The fat woman opened her mouth, as if to express her

approval, but next to her an old man bent over his stick snapped softly, 'Be quiet, woman! Now it's done. No triumph. Let's go.' Slowly, almost sadly, the crowd broke up and began to drift away, not one of them looking at the two murderers standing there with their pistols hanging from suddenly nerveless fingers.

The bigger cop cleared his throat. 'You gentlemen better be getting on your way,' he said, his voice revealing nothing, save perhaps sadness. 'I'll clear the—er—mess up. . . . Off you go, back to your unit before the enquiries commence.'

His companion, who had slipped behind the building to have a look at what had taken place there, nodded and held up two fingers, not taking his eyes off the dead Americans sprawled face-down on the rubble, the backs of their heads blown into a bloody fig-red gore, through which the shattered bone gleamed like polished ivory.

The bigger cop waved his hand at them as if they were naughty schoolboys in happier times. 'Come on, be off with you, before it's too late.'

Obediently the three of them turned and walked silently down the burning street, while the bigger cop watched them go, hands on hips, shaking his head sadly.

Two minutes later, they stood undecidedly outside the hospital's main entrance. Ambulances were pouring into the crowded courtyard. Red Cross sisters were running back and forth. Doctors, their overalls already patched red with fresh blood, bent over stretchers, heavy with their miserable human freight, selecting those who needed immediate attention. Over in the corner they were already beginning to pile up those who had been rescued too late, stacking them like logs. Already the pile of bodies was three metres high. Soon, they would be forced to ignite them; there were simply too many bodies for even a mass burial. It was customary.

The three of them stood in the middle of the controlled

chaos, bewildered and pale, seeming not to see the hurrying medics, gaping open-mouthed and stupid like village yokels visiting the big city for the first time.

For a long time they stood until de la Mazière said finally in a weary voice, 'We shall go back.'

Hanno von Heiter was too numb to be afraid. 'I shall die, Detlev,' he said without emotion. It was a simple statement of fact. 'We shall all die, *there*.' His voice trailed away to nothing. They were bringing in a little girl, still clinging to her doll, although she was out to the world, doped with morphia. Both her legs were missing. 'It doesn't matter,' de la Mazière said. 'Gentlemen, we go back to Russia. Come on.' He turned and started to walk away. Silently Hanno began to trail after him.

'Gentlemen,' Hannemann whispered to himself. 'By the Great Whore of Buxtedhude and Her Holy Pussy, I've never been called "gentleman" before. Things must be shitting serious.' But there was none of the usual exuberance in Senior Sergeant Hannemann's voice. He, too, turned and began to follow de la Mazière's bowed figure.

A minute later they had vanished back into the smoke, like ghosts returning to the grave.

Russia had them again.

CHAPTER 4

'GENTLEMEN,' Baron Karst announced proudly, as the officers and sergeant-gunners crowded around him on the parched field, the morning sun already blazing down on the steppe, 'we have our orders at last. *We go into the attack at fourteen hundred hours this very day!*' He beamed around at their bronzed faces as they squatted on the yellow grass, maps and notebooks at the ready. 'We have been given the great honour of supporting our comrades of the SS—General Dietrich's SS Panzer Corps!'

There was a murmur of approval from the greenbeaks who filled the ranks of the 1st SS Stuka Group and one of them called enthusiastically, 'Then we and our comrades on the ground will lead the attack, *Hauptsturm*? The SS is always in the forefront of the attack.'

'Exactly,' Karst agreed and indicated that the black cover should be removed from the map resting on the trestle-board at his side. 'General Dietrich's main thrust is towards the small Russian town of Prokhorovka from whence he will outflank Kursk and make an all-out armoured drive to link up with the thrust coming in from the other side of the salient. In the van General Dietrich will have the Bodyguard, mounted as infantry on at least one hundred of the new Tiger tanks, each one of them weighing over sixty tons and match for anything the Ivans can oppose them with.'

There were whistles of delight at the mention of the new secret weapon and the fact it would be carrying the most élite SS formation into battle.

'Then it's good night, darling, to Russia, *Hauptsturm*, eh?'

'I hope so,' Karst agreed.

'Yes, Karst,' von Einem, the veteran, said sourly, 'But remember the shitting Popovs are supposed to have *ten* times that number of shitting T-34s on our section of the front!'

Karst frowned momentarily. 'Admittedly, von Einem. That is where we come in. Even the Tiger cannot stand up to ten T-34s. One of them would be bound to get in a lucky shot. So we shall act as General Dietrich's flying artillery this great day. Naturally even we cannot knock out *all* the Soviet tanks. But we don't need to.' He smiled, pleased with himself. 'So far in Russia, we have been attacking on the basis that Soviet tank formations had the same sophisticated radio communications as our own armour. Intelligence now knows that is not the case. Only Russian battalion commanders—and perhaps squadron commanders, too—possess radios to link them up with higher headquarters. Those Slavic sub-humans have not got the intelligence, for the most part, to operate radios.'

'Yes, I know,' von Einem sneered, angered by the admiring looks on the faces of the greenbeaks as they stared at Karst. 'Six fingers on each hand and too stupid to count up to twenty unless they take their boots off—and all that kind of crap! But for Slavic sub-humans, they ain't doing too badly against our *so* smart generals of the Wehrmacht, are they?'

Karst flushed, but he was not going to be put off his stroke when glory and promotion seemed to lie in the very air. 'Let us stick to the point, von Einem,' he snapped. 'Once a Soviet tank unit is engaged, its primary means of communication between tank and tank is by flags. As Intelligence sees it, the Russian commander gives his orders to his subordinates, *not* by radio as our people do, but by wagging little flags like a damned short-trousered boy scout. And that is where we of the cannonbirds come in. We ignore all tanks save those where we see a Popov waving a flag. Take him out and their whole attack will fall apart. Without commanders, the Slavs, cattle that they are, cannot think for themselves. They will just run!'

Von Einem was still not impressed. He gave a groan and made as if he were pulling a lavatory chain and pinched his nose with the other hand. For him the whole plan stank.

It did, too, for Colonel Greim, standing with the newcomers in the shade of the field's only tree; he knew something that Karst didn't as he now plunged excitedly into details of operational heights, formations, refuelling procedures, ground recognition signals and the like. But he bided his time politely until finally, Karst turned to him, his face flushed and triumphant to demand, 'Have you anything to say to the men, sir?'

Greim nodded and reluctantly came out of the shade into the white glare of the July sun. 'Yes, I have, Captain Karst.' He stepped into the centre of the group, already aware of the steady rumble of heavy artillery to their front. The Russian positions were under fire, being softened up in preparation for the great attack to come. He looked almost sadly at his young eager greenbeaks, wondering how many of them would still be alive at the end of this week. '*Meine Herren*,' he said, 'first I would like to welcome back two old comrades, returned as if from the dead, von Heiter and Major de la Mazière, who now becomes my second-in-command once more.' Out of the corner of his eye, Greim noticed how Karst's face grew angry and knew why. The Baron was envious. 'Reluctantly, I also welcome back another old comrade, Senior Sergeant Hannemann. Though undoubtedly I shall regret his return in due course, insubordinate rogue that he is.' The sally was greeted by laughter from the noncoms and Papa Diercks called, 'Never fear, sir, I'll keep my glassy orbs fixed on the big hairy-arsed devil!'

Greim's good-humoured smile vanished. 'Comrades, as you perhaps know this afternoon's attack was intended as a surprise for the Popovs. Our armies usually attack at dawn. This was to be something new. But I must warn you,' he raised his forefinger, 'there is no surprise.'

'*No surprise?*' they called to one another and Karst flushed, as if he were personally responsible.

'No, and I shall tell you why. This morning at zero six hundred hours, just before dawn, von Manstein's forward

fields were bombed and dive-bombed—with severe losses—
by massive Soviet formations. His air crews were caught with
their pants down. Now it might well be our turn before the
morning is out. So I say this to you. From now onwards you
will be on five minutes' alert, standing by your aircraft,
fuelled and armed, and ready to go. We of the first SS Stuka
Group are *not* going to be caught on the ground. Clear?'

'Clear!' the answer came back in a hoarse roar.

'Good. Now remember, gentlemen, especially you greenbeaks, your aircraft are replaceable. You are not. Don't take
any unnecessary chances.' He took one last glance at their
earnest, eager young faces, here and there the more sober and
older ones of his 'peasants' who were still from the old days in
Spain and then raised his hand to his cap. 'Gentlemen, good
luck, I salute you!'

'Who are about to die,' von Einem said *sotto voce*.

Nobody laughed.

Now they waited, lying in the shade of their aircraft, faces
glazed with sweat, panting in their heavy flying gear, puffing
moodily at their cigarettes, talking in low dead voices; and all
the time the guns thundered with ever-increasing fury, as the
noise of the barrage rose to that final awesome crescendo.

To their front, stark black silhouettes against the blood-red
ball of the sun, the Tigers had already begun to move
forward, their decks heavy with helmeted panzer grenadiers,
turrets draped in huge swastika flags which would later serve
as recognition signals for the cannonbirds. Behind them came
the mass of the infantry advancing in slow thoughtful lines,
weapons at the port, as they waded through the yellow corn,
quivering in blue waves of heat. Then followed the assault
guns, the carriers, the trucks, and last of all, the boxlike,
white-painted ambulances, rear doors already flung wide
open ready to receive their cargo of human misery. All was
intense preparation and determination from horizon to

horizon as a whole German army moved into the attack. Only where the Russian positions lay, shrouded in the drifting brown smoke, interspersed by bright scarlet puffballs of exploding shells, was there silence and inactivity.

'You'd almost think the Popovs had buggered off, Hannemann,' Slack Arse Schmidt said lazily, as they slumped beneath the wing of de la Mazière's cannonbird.

'Yer,' Hannemann responded without interest. To his front he could just make out the red signal rockets shooting into the smoke above the Russian line. They were calling for help; they were suffering casualties from the barrage. But they were there all right. Trust the Popovs.

'What's up with you, Hannemann? Don't tell me an old shit-ram like you has gone and become a soft-shitter?'

Hannemann was not offended. Berlin and what had gone before during their escape had had its effect. 'No, not really. Just I've got crap beneath me curls about this one, especially after what the Old Man said earlier on. This new offensive could get really get into your knickers, old house.'

Slack Arse laughed easily. 'Talking about knickers, you perverted banana-sucker, what about them Berlin gash-merchants? I ain't seen a white woman in three months. What's it like, go on, give's us an earful before we start, comrade.' He leaned forward eagerly, the sweat dripping from his bushy eyebrows like opaque pearls.

But Slack Arse Schmidt was not fated to hear about his running mate's exploits with Berlin's ladies-of-the-night. Suddenly across at the makeshift control tower, figures were running excitedly towards the aircraft. A green flare sailed effortlessly into the burning red sky. Slack Arse flashed a look at his watch. 'Shit on yer quiff, Hannemann! It's still thirteen hundred hours—another hour to go. The balloon has go—'

The rest of his words were drowned by the first whine of the starters as Papa Diercks and his mechanics rose and began tugging away the chocs on all sides. Thin blue smoke started to stream out of the cannonbirds' exhausts. The first Stuka

engine burst into excited life. Suddenly the whole field shook
with noise, as crewmen flung themselves into the planes, like a
crowd of schoolkids boarding excursion buses, afraid of being
left behind.

In his new Focke-Wulf, Greim pressed his earphones
tighter to his ears to read the message being sent from the
tower. 'Recon reports massed Soviet armoured formations
heading towards the Bodyguard. General Dietrich has
ordered attack advanced one hour. Begs for immediate air
support.'

Greim was no longer listening to that excited voice.
Even as he rapped out his own orders to his subordinate
commanders, de la Mazière, von Heiter, Baron Karst, he
experienced that old sinking feeling: the knowledge that
things were going to go wrong. The Soviets knew everything!

Now they were rolling behind him, bumping and jolting
across the rough steppe, waiting for him, Greim, to take off, a
huge black wing of moving metal, packing more firepower
than a division of artillery. Veterans and greenbeaks, their
faces set and purposeful behind their goggles, eyes fixed on
the burning horizon beyond the massed ranks of infantry and
tanks, as they adjusted their controls, checked their instruments, waiting for that signal which would throw them into
the greatest tank battle that the world had ever seen. To their
front they knew the enemy observers would be watching their
sinister, black, gull-winged planes with the silver SS runes
and helmet insignia of the Black Knights. The Popovs would
know they were coming. But what did it matter? They were
the 1st SS Stuka Group. Who could stop their cannonbirds?
Greim, in the lead in his brand-new fighter, waggled his
wings and pulled back hard on the stick. The Focke-Wulf
lifted at once. Almost immediately it was sailing high into the
burning sky, undercarriage disappearing rapidly into its
sleek belly. Cannonbird after cannonbird soared into the air
to follow him.

They were racing across the steppe at 200 kilometres an

hour, dragging their black shadows over the upturned faces of the cheering infantry. The Tigers loomed up. Like massive black slugs they crawled towards the enemy. More panzer grenadiers rose from the decks and cheered wildly, hope and confidence written all over their teenage faces. Smoke shells began to erupt 200 metres or more in front of the leading Tigers. Yellow smoke streamed upwards, indicating the farthest extent of the German penetration. Beyond that lay the enemy. They raced through it. Momentarily they were blinded and came out blinking in the sudden glare of the merciless orange sun.

And then there they were. Packed from horizon to horizon, massed ranks of T-34s, advancing towards the Tigers, headlights blazing, dragging huge wakes of dust behind them. Tank after tank, an unending procession, so it seemed to Greim for a moment that the whole world was one moving grey metal mass. For one long instant he was too astonished to react. He had never in his whole life seen so many tanks. In comparison, the hundred-odd Tigers somewhere behind him in the yellow smoke were a group of pathetic little toys. But almost immediately he recovered himself. Zooming in low, ignoring the white curve of tracer already streaming up to meet him, he pressed his throat mike. 'To all,' he commanded, 'pick individual targets—*AND ATTACK*!'

The greatest tank battle in history was about to commence.

CHAPTER 5

IT WAS furnace-hot. The glare struck the eye like a knife. Above the stalled burning Tigers, the afternoon sky was the colour of wood-smoke, heavy with menace. Through it the sun glittered like a copper coin.

Sweeping round in a wide circle, gaze ever flashing back to the rear-view mirror on watch for approaching Soviet fighters, Colonel Greim watched as his pilots took up their positions. Below, the T-34s had halted, burning tanks filling their ranks, while the recovery vehicles jolted out from the smoke-covered Russian line to recover what vehicles they could from the slaughter of the First SS Stuka Group's first attack. But soon they would begin to move forward once more. Here and there, he could see the silver flash of a command tank's aerial as it moved about relaying instructions. If the Popovs pressed home their attack this time, Greim told himself grimly, they would break through the Tigers and slaughter the waiting infantry beyond. And the SS of the Bodyguard knew it. Already individual tanks had gone into the hull-down position, long overhanging 88mm cannon swinging back and forth warily like the snout of a primeval monster seeking out its prey. Already the great attack was beginning to bog down. 'Jaguar Two to Jaguar One,' the urgent voice crackled into his ears over the radio suddenly, 'Jaguar Two to Jaguar One. Do you read me? Over.' It was de la Mazière with the survivors of the lead group.

He answered promptly and de la Mazière snapped. 'Permission to attack now, Jaguar One? Have pin-pointed most command tanks to left flank by their aerials. *Permission to attack!*'

'Permission granted,' Greim answered at once and just caught himself in time from breaking radio procedure, by adding, 'and take good care of yourself, my boy.' He whipped the Focke-Wulf round again in a tight curve, momentarily blinded by the glint of the sun on the canopy, and turned to watch as de la Mazière formed his survivors up above the huge arrows of canvas draped across the parched, burned steppe pointing towards the Soviet positions.

With startling suddenness, they came racing in like black hawks. Twenty cannonbirds in a huge V, swooping in across the steppe, sirens howling like wailing banshees. Greim held his breath. This was it!

In the lead, Detlev de la Mazière came hurtling through the puffballs of mobile Soviet flak, feeling the plane being whipped from side to side by the powerful explosions, fighting the stick with hands that were wet with sweat, his shoulder muscles ablaze with pain, face contorted, teeth bared like those of a savage animal going in for the kill.

A command tank loomed up out of the fog of war. Its aerials lashed the air like silver whips, as it tried to escape, in vain. De la Mazière laughed crazily and pressed the firing button. The Stuka seemed to stop in mid air. It was as if it had just slammed into an invisible wall. Its whole structure vibrated madly. Then the first 37mm AP* shell was ripping the air apart, as it hurtled towards the T-34. De la Mazière caught a glimpse of the commander. Already he was trying to bale out, even before the shell had struck home. Too late! The solid-shot shell slammed straight into the command tank's turret. With majestic slowness, all ten tons of it rose into the air, turned a lazy somersault, and slammed into the ground twenty metres away. A gigantic smoke ring began to ascend from the dead vehicle. No one got out.

De la Mazière zoomed high into the leaden sky, already craning his neck to spot his next target, while Hannemann yelled frantically, '*YOU GOT THE WHORESON, SIR! YOU'VE GONE AND GOT HIM!*'

*Armour piercing

Stuka after Stuka was coming in for the attack, the planes spreading out like the prongs of a giant hayfork, cannon chattering, as the flak shells exploded all about them, weaving miraculously in and out of the bright red balls of flame. On all sides command tanks reeled to a stop, tracks shattered, engines ruptured, gas tanks already aflame. All was chaos, slaughter, noise, as a thick choking fog of smoke descended upon the killing ground.

Individual Stukas were coming in at ground height, seeming to skim across the burning steppe, hurtling from side to side, the flak missing them by metres, bearing charmed lives, cannon thundering, shells hissing in white fury at the stalled T-34s. Now everywhere the Russian crewmen, deprived of their commanders, were abandoning their vehicles. Others attempted to flee and in their panic crashed and smashed into each other with hollow metallic booms. Subordinate commanders trying to restore order, waved their little flags helplessly for a few moments before the air-gunners scythed them from their turrets mercilessly with vicious bursts of machine-gun fire.

Twisting and weaving crazily, flaps down to reduce their speed to almost stalling, the cannonbirds came in time and time again, mindless of the flak, hurtling through the fire-red mess of anti-aircraft fire, pressing home their attack with the bravery and recklessness of the good days, when nothing in the world had been able to stop the all-conquering *blitzkrieg*.

Now they were taking casualties. A crippled Stuka came racing in, trailing thick white smoke behind it. It hit the ground, sprang upwards high into the sky again, came down again with a terrible thump and stopped. The pilot walked out unharmed—to be mown down by a burst of Soviet infantry fire. Another roared down between two trees, its wings shorn off. Shakily the pilot emerged and staggered towards the cheering crews of the Tigers. '*Schnapps, bitte,*' he croaked, a weak grin on his ashen face. He got one. Next instant he fell down in a dead faint. But their casualties seemed to mean nothing to the bold, young men of the SS Black Knights this crazy afternoon. Time and time again, they came howling into the attack, cannon thumping, leaving behind them as they soared into the sky in a back-breaking climb, the black veil of mist already blinding them, yet a score more of crippled, burning T-34s.

The sight put heart into the younger panzer grenadiers and their comrades of the Tigers. Whistles shrilled. Officers waved their pistols. NCOs bellowed hoarse orders. The Tigers began to creak forward rustily once more, nudging their way contemptuously through the burning wrecks of their defeated enemy, while the bold young men of the infantry in their camouflaged tunics rushed the Popov positions, a cry of triumph and victory on their lips.

High above the killing ground, Greim watched the slaughter with no triumph in his heart, only compassion and fear: fear for his Black Knights. Soon the enemy fighters would appear. It couldn't be more than a matter of moments now. The Bodyguard had broken through, thanks to the First SS. Now they would have to manage on their own.

Yes, there they were! Yaks, fat-bellied, and stubby-winged, coming in for the attack in swarms, racing towards his boys. He pressed the throat-mike. There was no time to lose.

'*Take off!*' he shrieked into the radio. '*Take off! NOW! Here comes the opposition!*' Not waiting to see if the survivors were complying with his frantic order, he thrust home the throttle and raced forward to meet the new challenge, leaving the dead and dying to disappear below in the fog of war. *They had broken through!*

All that day and the next, the SS Corps of General Sepp Dietrich streamed forward, pressing the enemy backwards relentlessly, fighting for every metre, taking and giving casualties, leaving the way behind them littered with burning wrecks and the pathetic torn bodies of young men who would

never see their homelands again. The heat was tremendous
The sun streamed down mercilessly. Still the infantry slogged
on, uniforms black with sweat. The frightened peasants wer
forced out of their tumbledown cottages and made to sluic
the dust-covered marching soldiers with buckets of water. In
one place, their officers found an abandoned, horse-draw
hand pump and the locals were turfed out to spray th
crimson-faced bare-headed young men, working th
handles as if their very lives depended upon it. Which the
did.

All the while, the 1st SS Stuka Group flew cover for th
infantry, mission after mission, with the pilots in the air from
morning to nightfall, landing to refuel, re-arm, to douse thei
overheated bodies in great tubs of ice-cold water befor
dashing back to their waiting cannonbirds for yet anothe
low-level attack.

The battle intensified. On land and in the sky. A group c
young SS grenadiers were discovered, taken prisoner an
savagely beaten to death with clubs, before having thei
sexual organs sliced off and placed in their mouths so tha
when they were discovered it appeared they were smokin
some kind of obscene cigar of flesh. The news spread throug
the SS Corps like wildfire. A day later a group of youn
tankers ran amok in a newly captured Russian hamlet. The
drove the terrified villagers together, men, women an
children, and kicked them into the great evil-smellin
cesspool of the communal latrine, drowning them systema
tically in their own waste, laughing hysterically when som
shit-covered hand was raised in supplication from th
stinking mess, beating those to pulp who stubbornly refuse
to drown until finally they, too, disappeared below th
obscene mess of faeces.

It was no different in the air. Any pilot who bailed out stoo
the chance of being machine-gunned to death while he hun
helplessly in his chute, or beaten to a bloody pulp by the Re
Army men if he succeeded in landing and found himse

behind the enemy's lines. Twice, convoys of German wounded being trundled to the rear in long columns in clearly marked ambulances were shot up and bombed mercilessly, Yak fighters skimming across the steppe chasing individual soldiers attempting to flee the massacre. The 1st SS retaliated. Every village, the smallest hamlet, or individual collective farm which stood in the way of the advance was ruthlessly shot to pieces, whether it was of any military importance or not. 'It is give no quarter and expect no quarter, comrades!' Baron Karst briefed the weary young pilots, dark circles under their eyes by now, face ashen with exhaustion and strain. 'We are not dealing with human beings, people to whom we can apply European standards of conduct. We *are dealing with animals*! There is only one thing they can expect from us of the SS, comrades, and that is *sudden death*!'

Twice members of Papa Diercks' ground-crews were found stabbed in the back. In the manner of common soldiers they had gone wandering off the field, looking for something to 'organise', as they called looting, or perhaps for women. Soldiers would travel kilometres, even in territory lousy with partisans, if there was the prospect of finding a woman. In the end, after a third crewman had been tossed over the wire, with both his hands chopped off and his eyes gouged out, with the crude sign slung round his neck, *'DEATH TO THE FRITZ PIGS'*, Colonel Greim allowed an armed band under Papa to proceed to the next village, which still housed a handful of frightened women, children and old men, and burn it down to the ground. As a warning. But that night after Papa Diercks had reported to him that the mission had been successfully carried out and twenty-two civilians had been 'accounted' for, Greim had not slept.

Now all of them lived off their nerves, sleeping only when they were doped with cheap spirits or so exhausted that they could not see straight. The strain of combat was beginning to tell. Accidents began to happen and the faces at the mess in the evening started to thin out; more and more of the greenbeaks disappeared.

Von Einem was the first of the veterans to go. The night before he had been drinking heavily, his mood black and aggressive. Once Baron Karst had warned him he was drinking too much, but von Einem had snarled, 'You stick yer nose up yer own arse, Karst and not up mine! Don't worry, I'll fly tomorrow. Stick my face in the oxygen tank and I'll be all right, you'll see.' He had looked contemptuously at the monocled SS captain, with his affected riding breeches and stick. 'Hell, Karst, I can fly better *drunk* than you can fart into those fancy britches of yours when sober.'

Next day, however, the customary cure for a hangover— five minutes gulping pure oxygen from the great flasks used by the ground crews—hadn't worked. Von Einem had been leading in a flight of cannonbirds attacking a troop of T-34s when he had received an urgent warning by a forward ground observer that the Russians had a battery of flak guns concealed in a small wood to his right.

The rest of his flight had broken off their attack immediately. They knew, at the virtual stalling speed necessary for low-level tank-busting, they would be sitting ducks for the quick-firing Soviet multiple cannon. Not von Einem. 'Ah, shit on the shingle,' he had been heard to curse over the radio. 'Die proper and make a pretty corpse. I'll fix the shits' heels for them!' and he had gone flying on, straight into the concentrated fire of six anti-aircraft guns. His plane had disintegrated in midair. Afterwards, a volunteer patrol of the Bodyguard which had gone out to bring in the body—now they attempted to recover the corpses of all their fallen comrades to prevent them being mutilated—had been able to find only von Einem's ceremonial dagger with the SS motto which had been awarded him as a young cadet at Bad Toelz. Nothing else. His plane and his body had vanished.

Solemnly de la Mazière had had the dagger pinned up in the mess with all the other mementoes of comrades long dead, but behind de la Mazière's back, Baron Karst had sneered, 'The man should never been allowed to have joined the SS in the first place. Far too coarse and cynical. Absolutely no moral fibre whatsoever!' Then, as was the custom, they auctioned his kit and forgot Kuno von Einem.

Two days later it was Hanno von Heiter's turn.

CHAPTER 6

ON THE sixth day of the great offensive, Hanno von Heiter came into the 1st SS's makeshift mess *singing*! One of those absurd ditties he had used to sing when he had been brave and the old Squadron's comedian, about *'alle Mopse beissen, alle Mopse beissen, nur der kleine Rollmops nicht.'** He flung his cap carelessly at the hat-stand and called cheerfully to the waiting mess steward. 'Waiter, breakfast, please. Bright and beautiful—*cannonfire*! At the double now!'

And the waiter, grinning cheerfully, quickly poured Hanno his breakfast 'cannonfire', a double brandy. It was good to see the Captain so happy; he could have been the old Hanno von Heiter, the life and soul of the party as he had been in the great days of 1940.

Hanno tossed down the fiery liquid with a flourish and swaggered off to his waiting cannonbird, calling happily over his shoulder, 'Oh, waiter, I've packed my bedroll. It's clean.' He meant of pornography and anything else that might offend relatives back home. 'Auction off the rest, will you, old house?' And with that he was gone into the new dawn, leaving the waiter to stare open-mouthed at his slim back. Hanno von Heiter's actions were S.O.P.** but only *after* a pilot was dead. What was going on?

On the field, the sun's rays slanting obliquely across the parched, holed steppe and the guns already beginning to rumble at the front, heralding a new day of murder and mayhem, Hanno remained cheerful, but strange. Gravely he saluted Colonel Greim and wished him good morning, something junior officers no longer did at the front. Then he strolled over to where Slack Arse Schmidt lounged against their aircraft, drinking his morning beer and morosely

*All little dogs bite, only the little rollmops doesn't
**Standard Operating Procedure

chewing the end of a salami. 'Stand at ease, stand at ease, you old rogue,' he chortled, although the NCO made no attempt to come to the position of attention; they were all too tired for that now. 'Here,' he thrust a handful of mark notes into the NCO's greasy right hand. 'See if you can get the dirty water off'n your chest, if you can find a whore in this God-forsaken country. Or buy yourself a case of black market firewater and go on a twenty-four hour bender.'

'*Whore . . . twenty-four hour bender. . . .*' Slack Arse stuttered in surprise, peppering the air with bits of half-eaten salami. '*But what . . . where, sir?*'

Hanno von Heiter clapped the big sergeant heartily on the shoulder. 'I'm standing you down as my gunner this day, Schmidt. I'm taking one of the greenbeaks instead. Give you a rest. Besides a skinful of sauce might improve your aim in the future. God, you are a shitting awful shot!' And he walked away, leaving Slack Arse Schmidt still muttering to himself, staring incredulously at the handful of green notes, the equivalent of three months' pay.

Later he would gasp to his running mate Hannemann, or anyone else in the sergeants' mess who was prepared to listen. 'He saved my shitting life, you know. It was deliberate. Saved my shitting life!' And he would shake his big head in disbelief.

So Hanno von Heiter took off straight into the blood-red semi-circle of the sun peeping over the lip of the horizon, singing as he gained height that silly ditty about the 'little rollmops which didn't bite', bearing with him the unsuspecting greenbeak, unaware in his innocence that he had been selected for sudden death this fine July morning of the year of 1943. At seven o'clock precisely, the Group led by Hanno von Heiter's flight was alerted by the forward ground observers of the SS Corps that a massed formation of T-34s bearing infantry was approaching the forward elements of the Corps. Could the cannonbirds 'take them out'?

Greim said they would, but radioed it would have to be done quickly—one ground-level attack only—for Soviet fighter activity had been reported in the area and he was not prepared to risk his pilots on a morning which was absolutely cloudless, with not a bit of cover for his planes to hide in, if and when the Popovs attacked. It was the same order that he passed on to his pilots, as they flew at a speed of 300 kilometres an hour towards the approaching Soviet attackers. 'One run-in and one run-in only, gentlemen. If you make a balls-up of it, don't worry. You'll live to get it right another day. Good hunting!'

'And good hunting to you, old man,' Hanno von Heiter chortled back over the radio and increased speed, as if he were only too eager to get to the scene of the action.

De la Mazière catching that happy remark, frowned and asked out loud, hardly aware that Hannemann behind him was listening, 'Now what's got into Hanno? He almost sounds as if he's enjoying this.' 'With all due respect, sir,' Hannemann answered unexpectedly, 'he's like the rest of us. He ain't got all his cups in his cupboard any more. He's gone *meschugge**, like the whole shitting First SS Stuka Group!' Looking at his image reflected in the glittering perspex of the freshly polished canopy, he tapped his forefinger to his temple in the German gesture significantly, as if to emphasise his point. 'Absolutely, totally, blindingly, *shitting meschugge!*'

Ten minutes later they had crossed the German front and to the left had spotted the metal beetles of the T-34s rolling forward over the brown churned-up earth towards the SS. Behind came the infantry in their brown tunics, rifles at the ready, plodding forward steadily; for all the world like peasants crossing their fields, heading reluctantly for another hard day's work.

Greim reacted at once. 'Jaguar Two,' he meant de la Mazière, 'attack first!' he barked over the radio, eyes already searching the horizon for the Yaks. 'Then Jaguar Three.'

Karst smiled and acknowledged. It was the safest position. De la Mazière's group would catch the first packet of the Popov

*Crazy

flak. By the time he attacked, the Soviet gunners would be
nervous and uncertain, and Baron Karst did not intend to get
killed this day—or any other for that matter. To become a general,
his sole aim in this war, one had to play one's cards right.

'Jaguar Four, you attack last. If the Popovs become too hot
for you, break off the attack. Clear, Jaguar Four.'

Hanno von Heiter was completely unafraid. 'Affirmative,
affirmative, Jaguar One!' he answered brightly, his voice
sounding almost happy. 'The slightest smell of smoke from a
Popov popgun, Jaguar One, and we'll run like hell for home!
Over and out.'

'Over and out,' Greim said slowly, frowning like de la
Mazière had done. What the hell had got into Hanno von
Heiter?

De la Mazière flung a glance to left and right. Down below
the Soviet flak-wagons were already taking up their positions
as the T-34s scattered frantically, knowing what was to come,
the excited, sweating gunners throwing up the thin deadly
barrels of their multiple cannon to meet the challenge. Not an
Ivan fighter in sight.

Automatically he started to zig-zag and sway the plane
from side to side to put the Ivan gunners off their aim, while
behind him his Stukas lined up in the 'chain' for the sole run-
in, as Greim had ordered. Now the first, seemingly harmless,
puff-balls of flak fire began to explode all around him. Soon,
he knew of old, the whole sky would be peppered with
explosions. There was no further time to be wasted. He thrust
home the stick, crying, '*ATTACK! ATTACK! ATTACK!*'

The cannonbird fell from the sky. Suddenly he was carried
away by the old wild ecstasy, almost sexual in its intensity. He
was roaring in at 400 kilometres an hour, sirens screaming,
engine howling, every rivet of the plane shrieking under that
tremendous strain. The T-34s loomed ever larger. Wildly the
infantry on their decks flung themselves to the ground and
buried their heads in their arms like small children trying to
blot out a terrible nightmare. Tracer filled the sky like hail-

stones. Flak flecked it with brown and grey puffballs. De la Mazière didn't care. All he could think of were the T-34s, scuttling for cover like grey lice from underneath a log that had just been disturbed by an idle kick. A command tank swung into his sight. He hesitated no longer. He pressed the button. The Stuka lurched alarmingly. Just in time he caught her, exerting all his strength until it seemed his shoulder muscles would split the thin fabric of his black jacket. The white burr of the AP shell raced towards the tank. A commander flung himself out of the turret and ran for cover, his radio leads dangling from his leather helmet, leaving his unknowing crew to their fate. With the speed of sound, the 37mm armour piercing projectile slammed into the Soviet tank. The impact was tremendous. The whole vehicle—all thirty tons of it— heeled over, tracks still running like an upturned beetle, still waving its legs in death. Next instant it disintegrated, its tracer ammunition exploding, the shells zig-zagging wildly into the sky in multi-coloured splendour like some New Year Eve's firework display. A second later de la Mazière was zooming high into the burning sky followed by the rest of his 'chain', leaving behind them, at least, ten burning, wrecked T-34s.

Hardly had they gone when they were replaced by Baron Karst's group. Karst tried a different tactic, knowing that by now the Popov gunners would be jittery, uncertain, already wondering whether they should abandon their flak wagons before they were 'taken out' themselves. He outguessed them. Now whatever their officers shrieked about defending the T-34s, they would defend their own vehicles. Cynically Baron Karst grinned at his own image in the glittering perspex, as he zoomed in at tree-top height, heading for a bunch of stalled enemy tanks, crouched together like fearful metal animals far away from the protection of the flak concentration. 'Easy meat,' he whispered, lip curled in contempt. 'Easy meat'—and all good for increasing his score of 'kills', which would add the 'oak leaves'* decoration to his Knight's Cross and auto-

*A higher class of the Knight's Cross of the Iron Cross

matically mean further promotion. At 400 kilometres an hour, he roared in, fire button trembling under his forefinger, ready for the first safe and easy kill.

Two T-34s were hunched together under the pathetic cover of a grove of stunted pines. 'T-34s . . . wood . . . ten o'clock . . .' he called urgently to the pilot behind him. *'MINE!'*

Behind him the next man in the 'chain' cursed and sought another target, breaking right and running straight into a concentrated burst of 20mm shells, four barrels from a multiple cannon, firing one thousand shells a minute. The plane disappeared. Karst laughed and pressed home his attack.

It was the traditional milk-run, all the way. The crews abandoned their tanks in panic, flinging themselves to the ground as that terrible hawk of death swept in for the kill. They did not even attempt to fire the turret machine-gun. Karst took his time now. He lowered his flaps and, reducing his speed to almost stalling, he took careful aim. Once, twice, he pressed his firing button carefully. The cannonbird lurched under the shock. But Karst held the plane easily, not taking his eyes off the two white streaks of death hurtling towards the empty tanks. The first one reeled crazily. One track flew off like a severed limb. Thick smoke poured instantly from the ruptured engine. In an instant it was a blazing wreck, the sea of blue flame sweeping and engulfing the hiding men so that at once they were screaming, burning human torches. Karst almost clapped in childish delight. Next moment he had swept across the second one, feeling the Stuka shudder and yaw, as a tremendous explosion erupted below and the second tank fell apart. Laughing madly he soared into the sky, yelling his triumphant news over to a waiting Colonel Greim, who frowned and told himself that the ambitious Karst had picked the easy target yet once again. Nothing mattered to him as long as he saved his own precious neck and won promotion. Now there were no easy targets left. Hanno von Heiter would have to attack the T-34s bunched in the middle of the flak wagons, right into the jaws of hell itself.

Greim made a quick decision. The Soviet attack on the SS Corps had been stopped for at least this morning. They had done what they had promised. He pressed his radio button. 'Jaguar One to Jaguar Four,' he called urgently, 'Break off attack. Break off attack.'

There was no reply.

Greim swung his Focke-Wulf round in a tight curve, trailing white vapour behind him in the bright blue wash of the sky. Down below, one thousand metres or so, Hanno von Heiter was forming his planes up into the chain, out of range of the Soviet flak. He was going into the attack. Hadn't the young idiot heard? Was his radio on the blink?

Greim tried again. 'Jaguar One to Jaguar Four. Break off attack immediately! Break off attack. Do you read me? *Break off*—' The words died on his lips.

Hanno von Heiter had flung his cannonbird out of the sky. He was going into the attack!

He fell headlong. Greim and de la Mazière watched in despair and disbelief. Both knew what Hanno von Heiter was about. He was committing suicide. He hadn't a chance of surviving and he knew it. This was the honourable way out for an officer who could not cope with his fear any longer. Numbly they waited for it to happen.

Now Hanno von Heiter was hurtling down that chute of death in a crazy helter-skelter. The guns thundered. The air was full of bursts of scarlet flame and hard black smoke, as if some giant was peppering the sky with lumps of coal. On and on the cannon fired. Down and down Hanno raced. It seemed impossible that he could survive that tremendous barrage so long.

Already the rest of the chain had broken off the attack. The opposition was too fierce. Now they were hurtling to left and right, trying to gain height before it was too late. Hanno von Heiter flew on alone.

'My God, sir,' Hannemann breathed over the radio, voice full of awe, 'he's trying to commit—'

'Yes,' de la Mazière completed the unfinished sentence for

him, '*suicide*! That's it, Hanne—' Suddenly he groaned.

Von Heiter had been hit. He could see his cannonbird stagger as a red ball exploded under his right wing. Instinctively, the long years of training making Hanno attempt to save himself automatically, he tried to right the stricken plane. His right wing went fluttering down to the shattered earth below, turning over and over, first black and then pale blue, like a great metallic leaf. Immediately the cannonbird went into its final, impossible dive, engine screaming all out. The other wing was ripped off, carried away by that tremendous pressure.

Below the crew of the Russian flak-wagon which had hit Hanno's plane flung themselves over the sides of their vehicles frantically. The cannonbird was heading straight for them. Too late! The cannonbird smashed straight into it, rocking it over on its back. A second later both plane and flak-wagon disintegrated in one huge ball of violet flame, that sent a black mushroom of smoke rising higher and higher into the sky, as if it would never stop.

That night they auctioned off Hanno von Heiter's effects in the mess. There was not much for twenty-six years of life. A handful of newspaper clippings about his 'kills', already beginning to fade and yellow. A glossy official picture taken by Professor Hoffman* of Hanno receiving his Knight's Cross from the Führer. No one wanted them, naturally. A couple of tattered *Vie Parisienne*, dated July 1940, which an embarrassed greenbeak bought for a couple of marks. Fifi's lead which they decided, in the end, to keep in the mess with the other mementoes of dead pilots, where it would join the other trivia, which had once seemed important; the red-lace knickers, the English general's cap, the red star insignia, complete with bullet-holes taken from a shotdown Russian bomber, the French sign stating that 'all ordure was

*Hitler's personal photographer

forbidden to be dumped here'. A signed photograph, black stockings, top-hat and the works from Marika Rokk* which went for fifty pfennigs; and surprisingly enough a well-thumbed New Testament that no one could ever remember Hanno ever possessing. No one bid for it naturally and in the end it went for latrine paper (lavatory paper was short that week).

'Not much, sir,' de la Mazière said when it was all finished and the noise and usual cheers had given way to a sombre determination to get drunk.

'Not much, Detlev,' Greim agreed, nursing his *kognak* at the crude wooden bar, listening to the roll of the thunder outside which heralded the storm to come. 'Not much at all.'

The two lapsed into silence, while the wind rattled the shutters and to the east, the sky rippled silently with summer lightning, both preoccupied with their own thoughts. In the end Greim excused himself, knowing that they wanted to let their hair down and would not do so until he was gone.

One hour later they were all blind drunk, wrecking the furniture, taking their clothes off, shouting and shrieking, slapping and punching each other in drunken viciousness, all save Baron Karst.

Karst sat alone in the corner of the mess, listening to the hiss of the rain, nursing his drink and toying with his monocle, his arrogant face dark and brooding. Russia was slowly killing them all off. First von Einem. Now Hanno von Heiter. Soon it would be Greim. The Old Man had death written all over him. That would leave only that swine Detlev de la Mazière—and him.

He smiled softly to himself suddenly at the thought, as the storm raged and tossed outside, as if some God on high had determined to wipe out this cruel, crazy war-torn world for good. He would be a general yet!

*Wartime German actress

CHAPTER 7

COLONEL GREIM dreamed. He was back over Barcelona in the Civil War. In that blazing Stuka heading straight for the Red lines. The pain in his shattered arm was unbearable and his mind was electric with fear. If the Reds down there caught him, they would kill him—but slowly! As a member of the hated and feared Condor Legion, they wouldn't make his death easy. The *allemand* would have to suffer, *pero si*!

Somehow in his dream he escaped the usual castration and the ritual putting out of the eyes the fanatical *rojos* inflicted on their prisoners and he was back in the cave with Conchita, all flashing white teeth and liquid-black, worried eyes, and the boy Miguel, old for his years—and wise in that pinched, half-starved manner of his. As always, as they had done in reality back in 1937, they had tended him, fed him the best they could,* hid him from the Red patrols until he had become well enough to become Conchita's lover, a woman half his age. The age difference always embarrassed him—and continued to do so through the years when she and the boy had been his only support: the thing which had kept him going through these last terrible years; the only thing which made staying alive worth while.

But now the old, familiar dream was changing. He was still in that cave in the Pyrenees, where they had all hidden for so long, and Conchita and Miguel were still there, too. But they were in funeral black and Conchita was sobbing as if her heart were broken, while the boy stifled his sobs the best he could, as befitted a man. Why were they crying? Why?

To his horror, in the dream, he saw the cross they were

*See *The Black Knights* for further details

facing. It was one of those strange wire-and-enamel affairs, he had seen often enough in the hilltop cemeteries of the area, surrounded by the usual paper carnations. But whose was it? His frightened, fascinated gaze zoomed in onto the cross like a camera lens; and for the first time he saw the photograph curled in the glass jar at the base of the wire cross. *It was his own!*

Eyes still closed, he sprang from his bunk, fumbled for the water in the jug and splashed it urgently on his sweat-lathered, scarred face. It was only then that he dare open his eyes and stare at his old battered face in the flyblown mirror, the drops of water dripping down the cheeks like tears. He was still alive. It had been all a dream!

For a moment or two he stared at his image in the mirror, reassuring himself that he was *really* alive. 'Phew!' he breathed out, aware for the first time of the steady drum of the rain outside and the fact that for the first time in ten days there was not the usual dawn sound of plane engines being warmed up. Slowly he dabbed his face dry, silently renewing his pledge to Conchita and Miguel, thousands of kilometres away in Spain, that he would survive and continue to look after them. 'I shall come back, don't worry,' he said to himself in the mirror; then he began to dress, the nightmare forgotten, and prepared for the bloody business of the new day.

Outside now, it continued to rain. Lightning split the sky in scarlet flashes, drowning even the barrage of the heavy guns. Thunder rolled back and forth with an ominous drumbeat, while gusts of wind smashed against the tethered cannonbirds, shaking the six-ton planes, as if they were toys, as Papa Diercks and his ground crews, soaked to the skin, splashed from plane to plane in the ankle-deep mud, ensuring that everything was all right.

Inside the tight steamed-up mess, the mood was as grey and sombre as the weather. There would be no flying this day, in spite of the fact that the news from the front was desperate.

Dietrich's SS Corps was badly stalled, and all the signs were that the infantry division to the Corps' right was beginning to break under the weight of the Soviet counter-attack.

'And you know what that means?' de la Mazière said to the gloomy pilots as they gathered around the pear-shaped 'People Receiver'* to wait for the morning news. 'The SS Corps will have to withdraw and then everything will be in the pisspot. The whole front will have to withdraw. Thereafter,' he shrugged eloquently, 'God knows?' '*Obergruppenführer* Dietrich's Corps will never withdraw,' Karst declared, harsh and arrogant as always. 'After all, they *are* the *Waffen SS*!'

There was a murmur of agreement from the greenbeaks, straight from the training schools back in the Reich, but their expressions lacked conviction. All morning ragged, soaked men, still bearing arms admittedly, had been sneaking by the field shamefacedly, heading for the rear. They, too, knew the rot had set in at the front.

At nine o'clock, the news was preceded by the usual vulgar brassy fanfare of trumpets and rattle of kettle-drums which heralded victories and the excited enthusiastic announcer reeled off the details of the astonishing successes the '*Greater German Wehrmacht*' had achieved in the East on the day before: thousands of vehicles destroyed, hundreds of thousands of prisoners taken, scores of kilometres of enemy territory seized. . . . On and on he rattled in that bright, breathless, supremely confident style which had been pioneered by his master, the 'Poison Dwarf'.

But the victories did not impress his listeners in the tight, crowded mess in the middle of nowhere. For through the streaming windows, they could see another bunch of field-greys slouching by the perimeter, heads bent in defeat, one or two of them already without weapons. Even the greenbeaks did not need a crystal ball to know what they signified. The

*Officially-made radio of the times, capable of receiving only German stations

infantry division on the SS Corps' flank was beginning to break.

A disgusted de la Mazière was about to order someone to turn off that nauseatingly self-satisfied, enthusiastic voice when the confidence went out of it, far away in Berlin. Suddenly the brightness vanished to be replaced by a note of uncertainty. 'It has been unofficially reported by neutral sources, normally regarded as official,' the announcer said, almost hesitantly, 'that Allied troops have landed at two spots on the southern coast of the Italian island of Sicily. So far, no confirmation of these alleged landings in Europe has been received from the Führer's Supreme Headquarters. However—'

'*Sicily!* The surprised exclamation by a half score of pilots drowned the rest of the announcer's words. '*Good God!*'

De la Mazière flashed an inquiring look at Colonel Greim sitting quietly in a corner of the mess. He nodded silently in confirmation. De la Mazière bit his bottom lip. That meant Germany was fighting on two fronts again. Something would have to give somewhere. The Reich had not sufficient resources to battle the enemy to front and rear simultaneously. They would either have to capture the Kursk salient soon, or break off the action. There were no two ways about it. De la Mazière let his shoulders slump, as if in defeat. Had all the effort, the bloody sacrifice of the last terrible days been for nothing?

That afternoon, the rain still pouring down in a steady stream, it became clear, even to the greenbeaks, that the front had virtually broken. Just after Colonel Greim had announced the Group would be grounded for at least twenty-four hours unless there was an unexpected break in the terrible weather, a half a hundred field-greys, most of them without their weapons came slogging across the rain-soaked field, eyes wild and staring, crazed with fear, crying as they stumbled towards the buildings which housed the Group. 'The Ivans are coming! Save yourselves! The Ivans are coming, comrades!'

Peering out into the grey gloom, Colonel Greim recognised the signs. He had seen it all before. Once back in 1918 when the Imperial Army had broken and twenty-one years later in Spain when the Reds had collapsed. The front was about to break. Soon, perhaps even in a matter of hours, they'd all be running.

Captain Karst didn't think so. Followed by a handful of greenbeaks, he rushed out to meet the stragglers and deserters, face blazing with anger, slashing at them with that silly riding crop he affected, screaming at them to 'stop and fight like German men—not weak-willed women!' But his angry words had no effect. In vain, he and the greenbeaks stretched out their arms, like children playing some game in the schoolyard, and tried to stop the panic. It was only when Karst drew his revolver, and taking deliberate aim, shot a fat sergeant in the guts, that the rout ceased and a young officer—he could not have been more than seventeen— allowed himself to be led into the mess for questioning.

Bleeding from a nasty wound in his temple, his eyes wild, wide, and staring, he stood in the centre of the room, the rain dripping from his clothes on to the floor, while they looked at him, as if he had just landed from another planet. In the end Greim broke the heavy silence. 'Give him a drink, steward. The poor shit looks all in.'

Before the mess waiter could hand the infantryman the glass of cognac, Karst, his face crimson with rage, dashed it from his hand with a furious, 'Don't spoil cowards! The man is a traitor,' he cried, his eyes blazing. 'He deserves to be placed against the nearest wall and shot out of hand!'

Greim looked at Karst calmly. 'Captain Karst, for the time being still I am in charge of this Group. Not you.' Almost sadly, he nodded to the mess waiter who poured another drink. This time Greim himself handed it to the boy, while Karst looked on, his fists white-knuckled and clenched with suppressed fury. 'Here,' he said gently, 'toss that behind your collar, boy, and tell us where the fire is.'

Obediently the young second-lieutenant took the glass and for one moment de la Mazière thought he might burst into tears at such kindness. But he caught himself in time, gulped it down, shuddered violently, and gasped, 'There's no stopping them, sir! They hit us this morning—a single battalion—with a whole division of tanks. We were swamped. They rubbed out each of our foxholes, burying the men alive, crushing them to death, gassing them with their exhaust fumes, and we could not do a thing about it.' He shuddered again. 'It was horrible, sir! Horrible! Those of us who were left couldn't stand any more. We tried.' He looked desperately at the old Colonel. 'Honestly, we did. *We tried*! But it was no use.' He shook his head, a tousled blond curl swinging back and forth across his blood-encrusted forehead.' But there were just too many of them.' His shoulders heaved, as if he were sobbing silently.

Karst looked at him in absolute, naked contempt. 'A German soldier does not run away, man!' he sneered. 'He fights to his last bullet and last breath. Better death than dishonour!'

There was a murmur of subdued agreement from the greenbeaks. De la Mazière flashed Karst an angry look. But there was no stopping him. 'At least, we of the SS fight to the end. Better death than Slav,'* he declared proudly.

The deserter looked up, anger flashing through his tear-filled eyes. 'Big talk!' he cried in a broken voice. 'Big shitting talk, sitting here in a nice comfortable mess, drinking schnaps! What do you know, Captain, what it's like at the front?' His voice rose hysterically. 'Germany's lost the war in the East! The fucking slopehead Slavs have beaten us! Now it's everybody for himself. Don't you get it, Mister-so-brave-SS man. We're *all* fuckin' well hoofing it from the front. *Even*

---

*A wartime patriotic slogan, based on the similarity of 'Slav' and 'slave' in German *the SS!*' The greenbeaks gasped with horror. Karst raised his absurd riding crop, as if to strike the defiant weeping deserter. 'How dare you? *How dare you?*' he hissed, face crimson with rage. 'The SS never runs away!'

'But I'm afraid it does, *Hauptsturm,*' a thick Bavarian voice interrupted calmly. 'Indeed, I ordered two deserters from the Bodyguard shot only one hour ago.'

As one, the startled pilots turned and clicked frantically to attention, as they recognised the tough little figure dressed in a rain-soaked, ankle-length leather coat framed in the door, peaked SS cap set at his usual rakish angle.

It was no other than Obergruppenführer 'Sepp' Dietrich, the legendary commander of the III SS Corps!

'I know, I know, Colonel Greim,' Dietrich said patiently, as the rain continued to beat down and the shutters rattled with every freak gust of wind. 'That is why I came personally to make my own special plea to you, in spite of the fact that every hour I'm away from the front is precious.'

'But the weather, General,' Greim protested, indicating the nearest window. 'A pisspot couldn't fly in that kind of weather!'

Dietrich's tough brown face broke into a lined grin. 'I see we talk the same language, Colonel.' He dipped the end of his cheap workman's cigar into his glass of cognac. 'So let me put it to you like this. My Corps is basically in the bottom of the thunder-mug and any moment the Popovs are gonna piss on us. You see, the front is crumbling rapidly.' He gestured to the field-greys still plodding to the rear through the streaming rain. 'Another four—perhaps six hours of this—and it will break altogether. But there is only one chance of holding, perhaps even gaining the advantage once more—the positions at map reference 633 082.' He dunked his cigar once more and sucked it thoughtfully. 'One lousy bunker, armed with a couple of seventy-five millimetre peashooters. I can fart louder than them after a bowl of good old green pea soup, Colonel! Take them out and my Corps can advance again, cut right into the Popovs' flank and stop the rot.' He sighed suddenly like a man sorely tried. 'But there is no way that my boys can get close enough to assault the damned positions. Mines, concealed flame-throwers, barbed wire in depth, fixed-position machine-guns—the works! I've already lost the best part of a battalion of panzer grenadiers in the attempt. I can't ask my boys to try again. So what did I think, Colonel? I thought one—*one single*—cannonbird could do a better job than a whole battalion of infantry.' He pointed the wet dripping end of his cheap cigar at Greim suddenly, almost as if it were a deadly weapon. '*Just one lousy shitting Stuka!*'

Greim forgot the dream and that curled photograph of himself in the glass jar. 'Did you say—*one*?'

'I did.'

'Why one?'

'Because a whole group or squadron would alert the Popov flak. A single cannonbird could swoop right in, give the infantry below the signal it was going in, plaster hell out of those two damned Popov peashooters and my boys would do the rest.' He leaned forward, his tough Bavarian bully-boy's face hard, intent, compelling.

'Greim, you can't let me down. I'm about at my wits' end. There . . . there is no other way. As we used to say in the old war. This afternoon, Colonel Greim, it's *march or croak*!'

'So-so,' Colonel Greim said thoughtfully, pressing the tips of his fingers together, while outside the rain drummed down steadily, as if it would never end and General Dietrich watched him intently, the cigar smoking in a steady blue stream in his right hand. 'One single cannonbird. . . . *Just one pilot and one Stuka . . . so-so . . .*'

CHAPTER 8

OUTSIDE THE tractor bearing the 37mm shells ground through the mud. Beyond, a bowser pumped gas into the lone Stuka. An armourer fed in a long belt of gleaming yellow ammunition, the back of his overall. Papa Diercks, raindrops streaming down his face, his white hair plastered to his skull, doubled awkwardly back and forth, bellowing orders that were snatched immediately from his mouth by the howling wind. And in the door of their hut, the air-gunners, huddled in blankets and capes, watched in sombre silence.

It was the same inside the ops room as Greim bent over the maps with the Intelligence officer, their faces hollowed out to death's heads by the hissing white light of the lantern, while all around, the pilots stared at the Old Man with a kind of unrequited longing in their young eyes, as if they were watching the departure of a loved one.

Finally Greim raised his head and stared around at the stark young faces, white and strained against the black leather of their jackets. '*Meine Herren*,' he announced almost happily, 'you all look as if you have just pissed down your right legs. Let us have a smile in three devils' name, *please*!'

'But sir,' some of them began to protest, but Greim, still smiling, held up his hand for silence.

'I know. I know, you are all a lifetime younger than I. But the—er—Old Man isn't in his dotage—yet. I know, too, that you are going to object that I haven't flown the cannonbird so far. But let me tell you this. I was flying the good old Junkers 87* when most of you were still as high as three cheeses and still wearing triangular pants—wet ones, without doubt.'

*The Stuka

There was a murmur of reluctant laughter, mingled with more protests.

Again Greim held up his hands, gnarled with old battle scars, knuckles lumpy with the arthritis that afflicted all Stuka pilots sooner or later. 'It is better that I fly this mission alone as planned.'

'But sir,' de la Mazière protested hotly, 'the weather . . . the flak! How can you manage by yourself, without even an air-gunner?' Greim smiled at the earnest young officer with his handsome, hurt face. 'I've flown all over the world, Detlev, in weather that would make your hair curl—strictly by the seat of my pants. Besides this lousy storm will cover me against the flak. Hell, you know the Popovs? In this kind of weather they will have gone to sleep, I'll be bound.' His smile vanished. 'Thank you, gentlemen,' he said seriously, staring around, as if he were trying to fix their faces on his memory for all time, 'Thank you for everything.' He nodded to de la Mazière. 'Over here, please.'

Together they walked to the door, followed by the silent gazes of the others, only Karst's face showing any kind of emotion—one of deep, secret satisfaction.

Greim took de la Mazière's arm, and pressed it affectionately.

'Let me go, sir,' the other officer said.

'No, Detlev,' Greim answered, buckling on his leather flying helmet. 'If anything happens to me, I want you to take over—not Karst. That man has no heart. He is motivated solely by ambition. He'll sacrifice them all if necessary for promotion—and so many have died already.' Greim stared out of the window, the raindrops streaming down it like cold tears, as if out there he could see the silent passing of the young dead.

'Nothing will happen to you, Colonel,' de la Mazière said hotly.

Greim shrugged. 'Who knows? I've packed my bedroll . . . It's clean,' he added, using the traditional formula. 'No dirty

books. But there is a special to Spain. . . . Take care of it for
me, please.'

'Of course, sir. But—'

Greim stuck out his hand. 'Detlev, you have learned a lot in
these last months. You have changed, too. But learn this last
lesson.'

'Sir?'

'Germany is not only worth *dying* for, as you have been
told by your mentors of the SS.' He looked hard at the
younger man, eyes suddenly fierce and urgent. 'It is also
worth *living* for, Detlev. Think of that—*worth living for!*'

He opened the door and stepped out into the storm, the
wind whipping his grey flying overalls against his skinny
frame. Immediately the waiting NCOs doubled out into the
rain and stamped to attention in a flurry of mud. 'Sir,'
Hannemann, their spokesman, cried above the howl of the
wind, as further up the field Papa Diercks began to turn the
Stuka's prop, 'you can't go without one of us. Take one of us,
please sir.' Suddenly his big honest face was contorted with
sorrow. 'You can't take off without a gunner, sir.'

Greim shook the rain from his face. 'Now, what can I do
with an air gunner? Besides most of you hairy-arsed old vets
couldn't hit a barndoor, even if the weather was brilliant!
'Bout time they pensioned most of you old hares off.' He
smiled softly and took Hannemann's big paw. 'Thanks all the
same, you big rogue.'

And with that he was ploughing through the mud towards
the waiting plane, its engine already beginning to roar, while
Papa Diercks tried to fight back the tears that trickled down
his wrinkled old cheeks.

Savagely, de la Mazière slammed his fist down on the wooden
table, as the sound of the Stuka's engine was swallowed up in
the howl of the storm. '*Shit! Shit! Shit!*' he cursed, his face
contorted with a mixture of rage and frustration. Baron Karst

looked at him coolly, his mind full of wonderful plans. There were only the two of them left now. If the old fool didn't come back, one of them would become Group Commander. Even if he only became deputy to de la Mazière, it would mean promotion to the rank of major.

'What's got into you, de la Mazière?' he said calmly. 'Colonel Greim is only doing his duty as a German soldier and our senior officer. He knows what he is doing.'

'*Doing*!' de la Mazière snorted. 'Man, have you got all your cups in the cupboard? He's going to commit suicide out there. We shouldn't have let him go.'

Karst shrugged carelessly. 'What does it matter, de la Mazière? Do you really seriously think that Dietrich hopes still to break through, even if Greim does manage to achieve his objective?' De la Mazière looked at him sharply. 'What is that supposed to mean, Karst?'

'This. Dietrich is no fool in spite of his peasant appearance and background—he was only a sergeant in the Old War, you know? The offensive is petering out. But as a senior SS commander he doesn't want to be first to throw in the towel. If the Army runs, that's all right, but the SS must fight to the end—well,' he smiled cynically, '*almost* to the end. So back at the FHQ*, it will seem that the third SS Corps has gone on fighting till it was impossible to do so. Hadn't General Dietrich convinced a senior air force commander to fly a mission against the Reds in impossible weather?' He shrugged again. 'That's what I mean.' He sat back more comfortably on the hard wooden chair and smiled at an astonished de la Mazière.

De la Mazière stared at Karst incredulously. 'Is that . . . that what you think?' he stuttered.

'Of course. Times are changing, de la Mazière. One has to change with them. One has to be a realist, not a romantic old fool like our—er—*late*—commander. One still believes in

*Führer Headquarters

the cause of Greater Germany naturally and in final victory. But one cannot throw one's life away in absurd gestures. If I had been the Old Man, I would naturally have carried out Dietrich's request, but I would have sent one of the greenbeaks, eager for glory and a gong. But I would have been too much of a real . . .' De la Mazière was no longer listening to that cynical discourse. His mind reeled. Was it true what Karst had just said? Was Greim sacrificing himself for the sake of Dietrich's reputation? Surely he must have known, too, what the score was? Yes, of course, but he wasn't going to allow some stupid greenbeak, eager for glory and death, to waste his life on a pointless mission. My God, Colonel Greim was committing suicide out there to save the life of some idiot of a greenbeak who would be dead before the year was out anyway!

'It was about time that he disappeared from the scene,' Karst was saying, a cynical smile playing about his thin cruel lips, as he toyed with his absurd monocle. 'There is a need for new blood at the top in this Group, de la Mazière. Admittedly he was a good trainer. I won't deny that. But—'

De la Mazière sprang to his feet, his handsome face icy. '*Shut your damned fool mouth, Karst!*'

On all sides, startled faces turned to stare at him.

Karst's mouth fell open stupidly and he almost dropped the monocle he was playing with. 'What did you . . . did you say?' he stuttered.

'You heard me quite well, Captain Karst,' de la Mazière snapped, reaching for his flying helmet. 'Now listen to me—all of you. I am putting Captain Karst here in temporary command. With this proviso.' He raised his finger in warning. 'He can give you only *one* command in an emergency, and that is to withdraw under Soviet pressure. No other. I warn you—*all*! Any officer who obeys the command to fly an offensive mission, even if it comes directly from Captain Karst will face a summary court-martial immediately I return. Is that absolutely, completely clear?'

'Yessir.' The startled greenbeaks glanced from Karst to de la Mazière and back again, wondering what the devil was going on.

'Good,' de la Mazière snapped and finished tying the buckle of his helmet.

Karst sprang to his feet, his fists clenched, naked hatred in his eyes. 'I don't know what you are going to do, de la Mazière,' he bellowed, 'but if you are leaving me in charge, you can't give orders like that above my head! That is tying my hands! Leaving me—'

'*Schnauze!*' de la Mazière barked. 'I am still head of this Group in Colonel Greim's temporary absence and don't you damn well forget it, *Captain* Karst. Believe you me, I will not have the slightest hesitation in placing you under close arrest if you do. In fact,' he flashed the crimson-faced Karst a thin smile, 'it would give me, at this moment, the greatest pleasure to do just that. All right, Karst, don't just stand there like the proverbial wet fart waiting to hit the side of the thunderbox,' he commanded, enjoying Karst's discomforture immensely, 'get onto Ops at once and tell them I'm taking off.'

'Taking off?' Karst stuttered, 'taking off where. . . *sir*?' De la Mazière flung him a wild triumphant look. 'To find the Old Man, of course, and bring him back. . . . *To find Colonel Greim!*'

CHAPTER 9

COLONEL GREIM held on to the stick with all his strength. His eyes ached with searching. They felt as if someone had thrown a handful of sand grains at them. His shoulder muscles were ablaze with burning agony and the sweat poured down his face beneath the helmet in streams and threatened to blind him.

The weather was impossible. At times he was faced with a complete white-out and he flew blind. At other times the wind came crashing in at over 100 kilometres an hour, tossing the cannonbird from side to side as if he were on some crazy gigantic seesaw. In all his years of flying, as a young cadet in the Old World, barnstorming for five dollars a day in the Mid-West, flying through the tropical hurricanes of Central America for some greasy tinpot South American dictator, he couldn't remember ever flying in such weather. 'So much for flying by the seat of your pants, you old fool,' he said, hanging on to the stick, as the lone Stuka was struck by yet another furious gust of wind, the raindrops splattering the canopy to his front and momentarily blinding him. He banked and stared through the storm at the shell-torn ground below. Now, if his calculations were correct, he must be over the German front. Anxiously, his eyes narrowed to slits, he searched the sodden steppe. Yes, there it was. The crooked cross flag and a canvas arrow stretched out over the mud, pointing eastwards.

He came lower. Now he could just make out the tiny figures waving in their holes and the still shapes, crumpled everywhere which were the German dead. He was on target. Suddenly a red flare shot up to his front and hung there in the rain, spluttering and sparking in the wetness. He nodded

grimly. A forward Soviet artillery observer hidden out there
in no-man's land had spotted him, too. Already, he would be
working the handle of his field telephone, furiously trying to
contact the Soviet flak to alert them to the Fritz intruder.
Greim jerked up the stick again and the Stuka rose
ponderously, battling the storm, 'You'll have to get up a bit
earlier in the morning, friend Ivan, if you want to catch old
Greim,' he said to himself encouragingly.

Now he hugged the cloud base, as he circled slowly,
flashing glances to left and right, trying to spot the position
that was holding up Dietrich's SS boys. Now and then, he
caught glimpses of Soviet troops, bunches of infantry slogging
their way to the front, reinforcements probably, and little
columns of *panje* wagons bringing up supplies, once even a
long column of T-34s stalled and bunched together. They
would have made beautiful targets, but this day, he knew
there were to be no easy targets. It would be the position
Dietrich wanted taking out—or nothing.

'Why not—*nothing*?' the cynical little voice at the back of
his mind asked suddenly. 'Why the fuck are you flying this
mission—at your age? It won't alter things one fucking little
bit?' He nodded, as if in agreement, gaze still searching the
ground below.

'Besides,' the voice persisted, 'there's Conchita—and the
boy Miguel—to think about? Who's going to look after them
if anything happens to you, you silly old fart?'

Again Greim nodded. Still he did not cease his search.

'The whole damned National Socialist system is bankrupt!'
the little voice cried angrily. 'Why sacrifice what bit of life
you've got left for it, man. Haven't you got all your cups in
your cupboard? Can't you realise that?'

Greim sucked his yellow teeth, as if he had given some
thought to the matter. 'I'm German,' he answered the voice
aloud, gaze searching still. 'If we win, I don't think I want to
live as a German under that vulgar, monstrous system. If we
lose, well, what life will a German have under the Ivans?' He

shrugged. 'It is simply a matter of being realistic. My time, I think, has—'

'Don't be a stupid horned-ox!' the little voice interrupted angrily. 'What kind of shit-rubbish is that? What's all this German crap? You live because you are an individual, because of other individuals, the Spanish woman and the boy, if you like, not because you are a shitting German, man! Wake up! Get—'

The voice died away suddenly, was banished back to the furthest recesses of the mind from which it had come. *There it was!* The position that Dietrich had told him about.

Colonel Greim hesitated no longer, all doubts, all reason forgotten now. He threw the stick forward and fell out of the streaming sky. He was going in for the attack!

'There, sir,' Hannemann yelled suddenly over the intercom. 'There he is, sir! To port!'

De la Mazière swung his head round. There, through the flashes of lightning, he could see in a gap Colonel Greim's Stuka plunging downwards out of the clouds, with below tiny figures pelting for their machine guns and the first bright white tracer curving upwards in a glowing flurry. 'Christ Almighty,' he cursed, 'he's going in!'

'Of course, he is,' Hannemann yelled back. 'What did you expect him to do, sir?'

De la Mazière did not answer. Urgently he swung the plane round. Perhaps there was still time to stop the Old Man from sacrificing himself for nothing.

Colonel Greim felt again that old exhilaration, as he raced down towards the bunker. Even the electric flashes of the flak guns beginning to fire and the sudden puffballs of crazy smoke to left and right seemed exciting. He felt his heart beating furiously. Everything seemed clearer, more exact, more startling in detail. Now the tracer was racing up to meet him furiously. A shell came screaming towards him like a mad comet, dragging a long, fiery-red trail behind it. Instinctively he closed his eyes. It missed by metres, exploding harmlessly. He burst out into crazy laughter.

Now the whole world spun crazily. Furtively almost, his finger crept to the firing button. In the centre of that whirling landscape, he could see the bunker—a flat expanse of concrete, with its twin deadly guns emerging from the slits. It could only be a matter of seconds now. He tried to fling aside that wild excitement. He forced himself to breathe normally, though his nerves jingled electrically. Below him all was scarlet flame and smoke, stitched by the glowing, lethal morse of the tracer. *500 metres . . . 450 . . . 300 . . . 200 metres . . . 150*!

Gritting his teeth with the effort, he jerked back the stick. The cannonbird howled in protest. For one long moment, he thought he wouldn't pull her out of that tremendous dive—that he would go hurtling to his death. Then she answered. She started to come up, the engine howling furiously, the green needles of the instruments whirling and flickering crazily.

The strain was almost unbearable. He hung on desperately, the veins bulging a bright purple at his temples, his eardrums strained to bursting, giving off strange pop-pop noises, that red mist of old threatening to overcome him at any moment.

Suddenly he had her. She had levelled out. Beneath the flak, which was now exploding harmlessly in the sky above him. He gave a great howl of triumph. At 300 kilometres an hour, feathering back, flaps down reducing his speed by the second, he came in for the kill, the tracer hurtling towards him unheeded.

Now the bunker was filling his sights, growing ever larger, so that he could see every detail of the twin 75mm cannons, down to the pelting figures of their crews, rushing to take up their posts or flinging themselves to the ground in panic, as he raced over them dragging his evil black shadow across their quaking bodies. He gasped. It was now or never. He pressed the trigger. The Stuka shuddered, rocked from side to side, as if punched by a giant fist. For a moment he almost lost control. His cockpit filled with the acrid stench of burnt explosive. Then like a white thunderbolt, the first shell hurtled towards the guns. He pressed the trigger again. The second shell howled from his 37mm.

The Stuka raced forward again, freed of its load. The bunker loomed ever larger. For a moment Greim feasted his eyes on the sight, as the first shell slammed home, rocking the place to its foundations and crumpling the concrete as if it were made of icing sugar. Then he remembered his danger. In a moment he'd slap right into the place. He hit the brake. Next instant he jerked back the stick, tugging at it with both hands, the sweat pouring down his crimson face, eyes popping out of his head like those of a madman. A groaning thump. Another. And another. Below the ammunition inside the bunker was beginning to explode. Flame stabbed the smoke-filled sky. The Stuka rocked to and fro as if suspended at the end of an enormous swing, buffeted cruelly by that enormous blast, and then she was rising into the air once more, as below the bunker heaved and jerked, great dark cracks hurrying the length of its trembling structure.

'*He's done it, sir!*' Hannemann screamed shrilly. '*The Old Man's gone and shittingly well done it! I knew the old fart would somehow!*'

De la Mazière, wrestling with the controls as his cannonbird was slammed back and forth by the flak exploding all around him, watched fascinated, as Greim's Stuka emerged from the billowing smoke, stabbed by scarlet flame, like a phoenix and began to soar into the grey, rain-lashed sky. He had never seen such flying. Greim had been right. He could fly the pants off all of them. Now he'd done the job he had come to do, whatever the value of it, and had come through it unscathed.

Suddenly he felt a sensation of overwhelming relief. At that moment he could have burst out singing. Instead he broke off his run, hurtling the cannonbird to port and completely putting the gunners below off their aim. He pressed his radio mike. 'Jaguar Two . . . to Jaguar One. . . .' Then he flung all radio procedure to the winds. '*Well done, sir!*' he cried exuberantly. 'You certainly gave those particular Popovs a shitting bad headache!'

'Detlev? Is that you, Detlev?' Greim's voice came crackling metallicly over the air in clear, too.

'Yessir.'

'What in three devils' name, ar you doing here, Detlev?'

'Couldn't bear to be without you. Hannemann and I thought we'd take a little jaunt to see how you're getting on, and we note, you're getting on fine.'

'You know I could damn well court-martial you for this,' Greim began and then his voice lost its hardness. 'But I'm glad to have your company. Come on, Detlev, close up and let's take our hind legs beneath our arms—and get the living hell out of here!'

Now the two lone planes were racing across the Steppe at tree-top height. It was the only way to escape that terrible storm. Below them the sodden steppe zoomed by, devoid of life. They could have been alone in the storm, two metal birds flying away to a better place, leaving the war-torn world below for good. And all the while their radios crackled harshly as the two pilots chatted with one another excitedly, voices full of relief that the worst had not happened after all; that Russia would be soon over and they would be returning westwards to meet the new threat posed by the Allies in Sicily.

'Come what may, sir,' de la Mazière cried, as the raindrops lashed the canopy in front of him, 'I, for one, will be glad to see the back of Russia. I've had a noseful of the damned place! Let the Popovs have it.'

'That you can say again, Detlev,' Greim, flying only twenty metres or so away, agreed with a sigh of relief. 'It is clear now what the High Command will do. They'll pull back to one of the river lines and dig in there. If we can survive the summer—' Greim's voice broke off suddenly. 'Hey, what's that, Detlev?'

'Where sir?'

'To port!'

De la Mazière craned his head round. Out of the grey gloom, barely recognisible in the flurries of cold rain, there had appeared a long column of slowly moving figures, packed close together, with, for some reason, de la Mazière could not quite comprehend at that moment, their hands placed on their heads. Here and there in the column, there were riders in fur caps, wielding whips as they cantered back and forth on their stocky grey ponies. He frowned. They were German all right. He could see the field-grey uniform, mingled here and there with the camouflaged capes of the SS. But what were they doing down there, packed together, out in the open like that?

It was Hannemann who answered his unspoken question for him. 'Holy strawsack, sir,' he cried excitedly over the intercom. 'They're our boys, sir! Stubble-hoppers nabbed by the Ivans! They're taking 'em back to the cages, sir!'

Greim confirmed Hannemann's statement the very next second. 'Detlev, do you see 'em? The poor bastards have just been captured. They've—' His words were drowned by the sudden chatter of multiple cannon and 20mm shells started streaming up towards them furiously in a glowing, frightening, incandescent hail of fire. '*Flak wagon to port and starboard*!' Hanneman bellowed and swung round his machine gun, depressing it to fire quick controlled bursts at the twin flak wagons which had suddenly burst out of the whirling, windswept gloom and were hosing the sky with their shells, confident that the hawks of death wouldn't attack them in case the Fritzes shot up their own prisoners.

Hastily de la Mazière and Greim broke to left and right and jerking back their sticks sailed into the low clouds, followed by that deadly white fire.

'Did you see them, Detlev?' Greim gasped a moment later as the wet clouds embraced them and the flak vanished. 'There must have been over a couple of hundred of the poor bastards.'

'Yessir—and all heading for Siberia—*if* they're lucky.'

'If they're lucky,' Greim echoed grimly.

For a few moments there was silence, as the two aircraft flew through the clouds, dragging their shadows beside them, the minds of both pilots racing furiously, as they considered what they had just seen and what they should do. In the end de la Mazière broke the taut silence. 'Do you think we should simply buzz the column, put the shits up the Popovs and hope the stubble-hoppers have sense enough to hoof it while the going is good, sir?'

Greim did not answer immediately. Detlev flashed a look at the white blur of his face only metres away and sensed what might be going through the Old Man's head. All pilots were superstitious. By the very nature of their calling, suspended at the end of a piece of whirling metal high above the earth, they had to believe in luck, charms, portents, and all the rest of the foolishness, and all pilots knew that you couldn't draw on your store of luck indefinitely. It ran out eventually. Now the Old Man was telling himself he had been lucky enough to knock out the bunker and get away with it in spite of all odds. Could he pull off the same trick yet once again?

'Sir,' he said urgently, 'let me have a crack. I'll buzz them and you can take on the flak wagons from above, with your wing m.g.s. It would rattle them long enough for me to get in under the fire of the flak wagons.' He craned his neck once more and stared at Greim in the other plane.

For what seemed an age, Greim didn't move. Nor did he reply. What was going through his head at that moment, de la Mazière never knew, for he never lived to relate it to anyone. Then slowly, very slowly, Greim shook his head. 'Impossible, Detlev,' his voice crackled over the radio. 'More than likely those damned flak wagons will turn their fire on our lads when they make their break, if,' he hesitated and somehow de la Mazière had the impression that it took Greim an effort of sheer, naked willpower to complete the sentence. (Later he knew that in that moment Greim had uttered his own death sentence and knew it), 'we don't knock the whoresons out first. So this is what we are going to do, my boy . . .'

CHAPTER 10

'*STUKAS! STUKAS, Kameraden!*'

The cry of hope rose from a hundred hoarse throats, as suddenly the familiar howl of engines and the shriek of sirens that they all knew broke from the storm-laden sky.

'*Davai! Davai!*' the little yellow-faced guards on their shaggy steppe ponies cried enraged and swung their whips, cracking them across the backs of the nearest prisoners, cruel, slanting eyes full of sudden rage. But not for long.

As the first gull-winged shape hurtled out of the clouds, wing machine guns chattering frenetically, the downtrodden prisoners, who had hours ago abandoned all hope that they would see their homeland ever again, surged forward. They flung themselves on the Mongols who had been herding them eastwards, as if they were no better than the dumb beasts that they had once herded before the war. Savagely, ripping, tearing, gouging, they bore them shrieking to the soaked grass and trampled them to death, kicking their upturned faces until they were transformed into unrecognisable, hideous lumps of bloody gore. Here and there a desperate Mongol tried to gallop away, lashing the sides of his little mount in sudden, terror-stricken panic, only to be ripped from the saddle by a sudden burst of machine-pistol fire, as the prisoners seized their guards' weapons. Abruptly the whole long column was seized by new life, new hope. Cheers ran the whole length of the stream of prisoners, and orders, followed by counter-orders, went up on all sides, as the Germans decided what to do. How best to escape back to their own lines, as the second plane came zooming in at tree-top height, its machine-guns spitting fire, the slugs scything a couple of the fleeing guards from their mounts, leaving the panic-stricken horses to gallop on riderless, manes streaming in the wind, soaked coats gleaming with rain and fear. 'Don't waste time, comrades!' a giant of an NCO cried, hands cupped against the wind, face soaked and happy. 'Head west! To the sound of the guns! Before they bring up more troops. *Mir nach! SCHNELL!*' Plunging a looted bayonet into a Mongol who rose in the path and tried to stop him, he began to lumber heavily towards the German lines, waving his blood-stained weapon like a flag.

The rest needed no urging. A kind of panic set in. Crying and shouting wildly, the younger of the released prisoners took the lead, pelting against the rain, following the NCO, while behind them came their older comrades, yelling, 'Don't leave us behind, mates! Wait for us, mate! *Wait!*' Suddenly the whole steppe seemed covered by running figures.

High above the fleeing ex-prisoners, de la Mazière braced himself, as the flak-wagon to port started to trundle out of the grove of trees in which it had hidden itself during their first pass. Behind him Hannemann said, 'They're lowering the cannon, sir.'

'Aiming?'

'Yessir. They're gonna tackle the poor old hairy-arsed stubble hoppers.'

'What about the other one to starboard?'

Hannemann craned his neck. Colonel Greim's Stuka was hovering directly above it and as yet the crew seemed undecided: should they fire at the lone plane or should they cut off the escape of their prisoners. 'Don't think they know whether to piss or get off'n the pot, sir. It's neither one thing nor the other. But the Colonel's watching them.'

De la Mazière felt a cold finger of fear trace its way down his spine. Greim's plan was to keep the Popov gunners guessing until the stubble-hoppers could get out of range. But what if the Popovs made the wrong decision for Greim—and fired at him? He'd be a sitting duck hovering at that height. 'Hold on to your hat, Hannemann. We're going in. *NOW!*'

He threw the Stuka out of the sky, sirens howling frenetically, engine going all out.

The Russians to port reacted instinctively. The gun-aimer threw up his four slim cannon mounted on the back of an open truck and pressed his trigger. Bright angry lights flashed all around the crazily diving plane. A string of glowing coals that were 20mm shells rippled upwards. De la Mazière dived regardless, face set and tense. He roared through a burst of shellfire. His acceleration was tremendous. Already he could feel himself gasping for breath as if he were running a great race and a thin trickle of black blood had begun to escape from his distended nostrils. Down and down he roared. He hit the fire button, and levelled out in the very same instant that the Stuka took a tremendous burst of shrapnel.

The plane trembled violently like a suddenly trapped wild animal. Abruptly de la Mazière's bleeding nostrils were assailed by the acrid stink of torn metal, cordite and burnt rubber. Blood spurted from his right leg. In a flash he felt his toes curl up into a glutinous warm mess, as cold air poured in through a score of holes.

'We've been hit!'

'The flak wagon's bought it, sir!' Hannemann shrieked, ignoring de la Mazière's remark. 'Look at the sonuvabitch! You've really brewed her up, sir!'

He had. The whole length of the flak-wagon was a sea of scarlet flame, with white tracer shells zig-zagging crazily into the air in all directions, as the guns' ammunition exploded in that tremendous heat. Next to it, burning gunners writhed miserably in the smoking grass. Groggily de la Mazière pulled back on the stick, while below the running men, faces turned upwards, stopped and cheered madly. He saw them double. He fought off the blackness which threatened to swamp him. Slowly, very slowly, he brought the crippled plane round, thick black smoke pouring from it, its engine giving off strange, alarming hiccups, as if it might cut out at any moment.

'*Detlev!*' Greim cried as below him the second flak-wagon scurried round, turning its cannon in the direction of the crippled plane, limping along at tree-top height, sensing an easy kill. '*No, Detlev, not you!*'

For one long moment Conchita's beautiful face and that of the boy Miguel flashed before his mind's eye and he could not bring himself to do what he knew he had to do. Below the second flak wagon had slammed to a stop and the gunner was raising his cannon furiously. At that range, he couldn't miss. Detlev's Stuka was flying just above stalling speed and Greim could see he had no chance of manoeuvring. He dismissed the two of them, the only ones he loved in this sorry world. '*Vaya con Dios,*' he said softly and threw forward the stick.

There was no time to aim. As he fell out of the sky at 400 kilometres an hour, Greim knew with the absolute clarity of a vision, that he was flying his last mission. There was only one way to knock out that Popov flak-wagon before it shot Detlev's crippled plane out of the sky.

Now the flak-wagon was centred plumb in the middle of his cockpit. It was a perfect target. But the gunner had already begun to whirl his wheels, Detlev's plane in his sights obviously—and he, Greim, might miss with his own gun. He gritted his teeth and urged the plane forward at ever greater speed. Now he was sliding down that final tunnel with death at its exit. There was no other way.

Far far away, he could hear Detlev de la Mazière's voice faint but understandable, 'Don't sir,' it urged wearily. 'Please don't. I'll make it. Hannemann will.' The voice trailed away into nothingness and he no longer heard. His whole being was concentrated on that flak-wagon. He hurtled towards it as if mesmerised. It seemed to fill his whole world. Cold beads of sweat broke out on his forehead, as he realised what he had to do. Bitter bile flooded his throat. *But there was no other way!*

A burst of m.g. fire hit the canopy. The wall of perspex splintered into a hundred dull stars. Black oil began to spread over it. He rolled over on his back, the only tactic he could think of, to clear away the oil. He had his excuse. The Stuka was hit. He could break off the attack. But even as the wind and the rain washed away the oil and he could see again, he knew that he wouldn't. Fate had ordained that he would carry out this last mission. His whole life had been leading up to this final overwhelming moment. He gripped the stick with renewed purpose and let it happen.

Hannemann winced as the Old Man's Stuka slammed into the flak wagon at 400 kilometres an hour. For a moment, the two of them, the flak-wagon and the plane, slithered across the soaked steppe, while the troops fled ever closer to their own lines. Then abruptly the Stuka and the flak wagon exploded simultaneously. Red flame seared the steppe like a giant blow-torch. Even at that distance, he felt the explosion. It was as if some giant hand was squeezing his guts. A monstrous funeral pyre of bright scarlet flame shot to the grey sky and for an instant the whole of the steppe appeared to be on fire. Next moment it was gone and all that remained below was a grotesquely twisted pile of glowing metal. No one got out.

Gently Hannemann pressed the button of his intercom. 'Sir?'

It seemed to take the wounded pilot in front of him an age to answer. 'Yes, Hannemann,' de la Mazière croaked finally. 'Did he?'

'Yessir.'

'And the Old Man?'

'Colonel Greim, sir . . .' Hannemann's voice threatened to break but he caught himself just in time. 'Bought it, sir.'

'I see. . . . Well, I suppose it's time to go home, isn't it?' Wearily he fixed his gaze on the shattered controls. Like a wounded animal, the crippled plane started to limp westwards. A moment or two later it had disappeared into the leaden clouds, a thin trail of rapidly disappearing black smoke all that marked its passing.

EPILOGUE

Envoi

DARK SQUAT dots stretched the whole length of the heaving horizon. Beyond, a series of scarlet, silent volcanoes erupted. A squadron of two-engined bombers screamed in low above the invasion fleet, raced across the white beach, to drop their loads in the lemon-groves further inland. The huge 16-inch shells from the battle-wagons beyond the horizon shrieked in above the heads of the infantry in the barges and exploded in showers of sand the length of the beach exits. To the unseen watchers in the clouds, they looked for all the world like a line of dancing chorus girls.

Now the first barges were breasting the surf with their blunt ugly noses, their screws churning up the water to a dirty cream. Soon their ramps would be lowered and the infantry would begin fanning out, to pelt up the wet sand. Behind them the tank-landing craft were preparing to come in with the next wave. Standing on the bridges of the command ships, the high-ranking officers in their dome-shaped, lacquered helmets and watching through expensive binoculars, nodded their approval. Everything was going according to plan. Here and there an officer shook the hands of his fellows, as if in self-congratulation. This first landing on the soil of Hitler's vaunted 'Fortress Europe' was going to be totally unopposed.

Closer and closer the first line of barges came to that deserted beach, each clumsy craft trailing a dirty white V behind it, the crouched infantry wet and cold, but confident, their well-fed young American faces glowing with energy. What could stop this mighty armada from God's Own Country now? Another squadron of Mitchell bombers hurtled across the invasion fleet to add their bombs to the smoking burning mess further inland. Now the seamen were beginning to lower the ramps. Above the rattle of the rusty chains, young infantry officers, faces set and determined underneath their dome-shaped helmets, rapped out orders through their megaphones. In a minute more they would be going in. 'Somewhere a sturdy voice started to sing lustily, *'Over there, over there! For the Yanks are coming. . . . Over there, have a care . . . for the Yanks are coming. . . .'*

'Give 'em hell, Yanks!' the English sailors who manned the barges called cheerfully, knowing they were going back to the big ships.

'Attaboy, limey!' the infantry yelled back and gripped their Garands more tightly.

Whistles shrilled. 'Stand by, guys!' the young officers commanded.

'This is it, fellahs!' the excited young GIs cried. *'Buon giorno!'* a wag yelled.

The ramps were almost in the water now. The engines had stopped. The barges were drifting through the last of the surf. The white, perfectly empty beach was only yards away. Now the waiting infantry could smell the land, a mixture of wild thyme, pine resin and smoke from the burning hilltops. They had almost done it. Nothing, *but nothing*, could stop them now. They were landing in Italy, and the Krauts were going to be able to do absolutely nothing about it. The young officers dropped their megaphones, gripped their carbines more firmly, and rose to their feet so that their young soldiers could see them. 'K fellahs,' they yelled jauntily, *'Now, let's hit that beach!'* They surged forward. *'Let's go. . . .'*

Hovering high in the sky, mere black dots above the unsuspecting invaders from the New World, the Hawks of Death waited, circling in slow sinister curves. Round and round they went in their lazy circles, stark and silent against the burning blue wash of the Italian sky. Below the toy boats began to discharge their human cargo. Tiny black figures struggled against the surf as they clambered to that brilliant

white beach. Beyond the smoke rose in black mushrooms, as
the fleet pounded the interior—purposelessly; for the German
Army had long withdrawn northwards. The Americans were
punching into an empty bag.

'Look at em, sir,' Hannemann said, as he craned his neck to
look downwards. '*Amis!* They must breed 'em like rabbits
over there in the land of boundless possibilities. Shit on the
shingle—they're everywhere!'

Colonel de la Mazière, the new commander of the 1st SS
Stuka Group, did not answer. He was watching the invaders
with the intensity of a bird-of-prey waiting for the right
moment to pounce on its unsuspecting victim. How orderly
and well-organised everything down there looked? The
steady lines of ships, carefully spaced out; the exact positioning
of the landing barges so that the infantry could get ashore
with nothing more than wet feet; the artillery support from
the battle wagons, well concealed out at sea beyond the
horizon. All was as could be expected from the world's
greatest industrial power, moving with precise factory-
efficiency. Surely nothing could stop that khaki-clad machine?

'Willyer cast your glassy orbs on the confident shits,'
Hannemann said with a bitter note of envy in his voice now,
'they're sitting down on the beach now, as if they're gonna
have a shitting picnic! They look as if they're even taking off
their dice-beakers to dry their shitting feet.' He shook his
head in mock disbelief. 'In a minute they'll be landing a
shitting brass band—to serenade the confident, young
asparagus Tarzans!'

As if on cue, the sun flashed on gleaming silver and a mass
of tiny figures clasping brightly polished instruments began to
struggle through the surf to the men cheering them on, on the
beach.

Hannemann clapped his hand to his forehead, as if he
could not believe the evidence of his own eyes, and gave a low
groan. De la Mazière smiled thinly, but there was no
answering light in those hard blue eyes of his. They remained

icy, calculating, and empty of any emotion save the desire to inflict hurt, to kill. How old and cynical he felt at that moment, his youth had vanished in these last terrible years of war! Now came these new enemies, full of the energy and confidence of young men who had never been in battle. Soon they must learn to pay the price of that youthful confidence. In a moment, he must present them with the butcher's bill.

Colonel de la Mazière checked his instrument panel for one last time and pressed his throat-mike. 'Jaguar One—to all,' he commanded, voice expressionless, face without emotion, 'prepare to attack.' With his free hand, he pushed down his goggles, '*ATTACK*!' '*Sieg Heil*! *Sieg Heil*!' came back the excited cries of the greenbeaks, as the planes lined up in the chain.

Colonel de la Mazière clicked off the radio. He had no time for such foolishness now. For one more moment he hovered there in that burning blue sky, selecting his target, the men he would kill in the next moment, and then he flung the stick forward. The nose dipped. His Stuka dropped out of the sky and that old exhilarating race of death began yet again.

Behind him Senior Sergeant Hannemann screamed, as he twisted his gun round and prepared to slaughter the khaki-clad innocents below, '*WELCOME TO EUROPE, BOYS*!'